成語學英文

張學明 編著

U0106905

商務印書館

成語學英文

作　　者　張學明

責任編輯　黃家麗

裝幀設計　涂　慧　黎奇文

出　　版　商務印書館（香港）有限公司
　　　　　香港筲箕灣耀興道 3 號東滙廣場 8 樓
　　　　　http://www.commercialpress.com.hk

發　　行　香港聯合書刊物流有限公司
　　　　　香港新界大埔汀麗路 36 號中華商務印刷大廈 3 字樓

印　　刷　美雅印刷製本有限公司
　　　　　九龍觀塘榮業街 6 號海濱工業大廈 4 樓 A 室

版　　次　2019 年 2 月第 1 版第 1 次印刷

I am over the moon to have been invited by Professor Fred Cheung to contribute this Foreword. An idiom is a collection of words that have a meaning that goes beyond the literal meaning of the individual words. For writers, idioms add depth and breadth to their expression. For readers, the texture and colour of the message takes on a different dimension, beyond the mere expression of words. For language lovers, the implied meaning behind idioms enriches the text.

Having enjoyed a friendship with Professor Cheung for over 20 years, I can speak highly of his considerable knowledge. He draws on this to help us understand not only the meaning implied by idioms, but also to better understand the history and stories that these short expressions stem from. As an expert in history and mythology, and being conversant in several languages, he is best positioned to collate this book. It will be a handy reference for all who are keen to fathom the depths of English. If learners of English wish to enhance their love of the language, this is the book for them.

Lester G Huang, SBS JP

Lester G Huang is the Chairman of the Standing Committee on Language Education and Research, and the Chairman of the Council of the City University of Hong Kong.

我很榮幸獲得張學明教授邀請替他的新書《成語學英文》撰寫前言。成語 (idiom) 是一組詞彙，而它們的意義比較個別的文字意思深入得多。對寫作人而言，成語可以令他們的表達更深更廣。對讀者而言，成語的韻味與色彩又有另一不同角度，遠遠超越一般文字的表達。對語文愛好者而言，成語背後的內涵意義充實了文章。

張教授和我是二十多年的好朋友，我高度評價他的廣博學識。他的新書帶領我們去了解不只是成語的意思，而是更令我們認識成語背後的歷史和故事。張教授是歷史、神話及多種語文的專家，他是出版這本書的最合適人選。讀者若希望追尋英語更深層次的內涵，這本書會是最方便的參考。英語學生若想提升他們對語文之愛好，這本書就是為他們而寫的。

黃嘉純 SBS JP

黃嘉純先生是語文教育及研究常務委員會主席及香港城市大學校董會主席。

筆者研讀古希臘文、拉丁文、法文、翻譯學、字源學、英國中古史（博士論文），並教授西洋上古史、中古史、中西神話、英國早期憲法史、西方文化的特質、中國通史等科目三十多年，深信透過追溯中西方的經典字源、成語、名人名句、俚語及其故事，探討中西方歷史、文化，可以增強讀者的中英文詞彙，並讓他們更深入了解及掌握中西方文明，包括理念和價值觀，及歷史文化的知識，甚至提高中英語文及翻譯的造詣，所以筆者決定編著這本《成語[1] 學英文》。

西方文化之典故往往根源於《聖經》、古希臘和羅馬神話、《伊索寓言》、古希臘文、拉丁文，甚至法文；中國文化之典故則多源於四書五經、古籍如《戰國策》及後期的《史記》、《三國》、唐宋詩詞等，因此，本書會提供這些典故、名人名句、成語、詩詞，附上相關的古希臘文、拉丁文、中英文翻譯，又追溯背後有趣的故事與延伸字彙，內容和我們日常生活關係密切，既增長知識又趣味盎然。

本書以英文字母順序排列 (alphabetical order)，方便讀者查閱。

張學明

1　本書的"成語"，除了一般四字成語之外，亦包括多字成語，例如《伊索寓言》的諺語及中外古今之名人名句、俚語等。

首先感謝我的家人及師生好友鼓勵我編寫這本書，感謝香港
商務印書館替我出版，也要感謝我的老師，包括希臘文、拉丁
文、法文、英文、中文、翻譯及博士論文的指導教授，他們
令我對中西成語、典故及歷史故事有很多啟發和更深入的了
解。最後，要感謝黃嘉純先生 (Mr. Lester Garson Huang, SBS
JP) 替這本書撰寫前言，在此衷心感謝各位！

CONTENTS 目錄

凡帶圖標 🔁 表示：參看張學明《字源學英文》(香港：商務，2017)
用方括號注釋古英語

A bird in (the) hand is worth two in the bush
一鳥在手勝於百鳥在林

此英文成語的意思是要珍惜所有，不要因為渴望取得更好的東西而放棄已擁有之物。人若希望得到更多而放棄手上已有的東西，他們就是愚昧的。(Men are foolish who, in hope of more, let those, which they have in their hand go.)

參看
REFERENCE

Hugh Rhodes, The Boke [Book] of Nurture or Schoole [School] of Good Maners [Manners]. (1530): "A byrd [bird] in hand – is worth ten flyes [flies] at large."

John Heywood, glossary A Dialogue *Conteinyng the Nomber in Effect of All the Prouerbes in the Englishe Tongue*. [*A Dialogue Containing the Number in Effect of All the Proverbs in the English Tongue*] (1546): "Better one byrde [bird] in hande [hand] than ten in the wood."

你知道嗎
DO YOU KNOW?

《伊索寓言》裏有一個 "夜鶯與鷹" 的故事 (Aesop's Fables, "The Nightingale and the Hawk") :

一隻飢餓的鷹看見一隻夜鶯，鷹飛下並捉住夜鶯。夜鶯哀求鷹不要吃牠，指森林裏有很多更大的鳥，鷹回答道："你已經在我手中，若我放了你而想着去森林捉更多 (兩隻甚至百隻) 鳥，我便是很愚蠢的了！" 這個寓言教訓我們：不要因幻想更多未捉到或未掌握的，而放走那些已捉到和控制得到的。

例子
EXAMPLES

Henry has many girlfriends at the same time. Some friends advise him to choose one and be faithful to her – "**a bird in the hand is**

worth two in the bush!"（亨利同一時間有多個女朋友，一些朋友忠告他：盡快選一個，不要再三心兩意 ─ "一鳥在手勝於百鳥在林"啊！）

A black sheep (of the family)
害羣之馬

Bad apples / Rotten apples / A rotten apple in the barrel /
A disgraced member in the family

此英文成語的意思是個人的行為或質素不好，引致一個羣體受到損害。中文也有類似的成語，如害羣之馬。

你知道嗎
DO YOU KNOW?

據說遠古時，軒轅黃帝去鄉村看望他的一個朋友。路上，他遇到一個看守馬羣的男孩。黃帝問男孩："你知不知道村莊的路呢？那兒住着我的一個朋友。"男孩說知道。黃帝又問男孩："認不認識我的朋友？"男孩回答認識。黃帝又問他："你知道怎樣治理國家嗎？"男孩說："治理國家和看守一羣馬差不多 ─ 只要把害羣之馬從馬羣裏趕走就行了。"

例子
EXAMPLES

Professor Warren Hollister (1930-1997) was a world-renowned historian on medieval English history at the University of California, Santa Barbara. He had supervised 29 PhDs – all have been professors at various universities. Among the 29 PhDs, Dr. Fred Cheung (author of this book) was the only Chinese. One day, Fred asked Professor Hollister if he was "**the black sheep of the family**." Professor Hollister answered, "No! Of course not! Frederick, you are really good, I am proud of you! Keep your chin up!" (Professor Hollister (1930-1997) 是加州大學著名的英國中古史教授，他指

導過 29 位博士 (全都是大學教授)，但只有張學明 (筆者) 是中國人。有一天，筆者問師傅自己是否師門的害群之馬 **(the black sheep of the family)**。Professor Hollister 回答道："當然不是！您真的很好，我以您為榮！挺起胸膛吧！")

A blessing in disguise
禍福倚伏

Mixed blessing / 塞翁失馬，焉知非福

此英文成語的意思，是一些看來不好的事情，到最後可能有意想不到的好處，就像是隱藏的祝福。中文也有類似的成語，如禍福倚伏，意思是福氣可以變成禍患，禍患也可以變成福氣，沒有一個絕對的定論。

★ 參看
REFERENCE

《史記‧屈原賈生列傳》："禍兮福所倚，福兮禍所伏，憂喜聚門兮，吉凶同域。"

▲ 你知道嗎
DO YOU KNOW?

道家亦有類似的哲學思想，其實這句中文成語，可能正是出於道家的："禍福倚伏，幽微難明，禍兮福所倚，福兮禍所伏"。在《淮南子‧人間訓》裏有這樣的故事：

靠近邊塞的地方，有一位精通術數的人。他家的馬自己跑到胡人那邊去了，大家都來慰問他，他說："可能是福呢？"過了幾個月，他家的馬帶了一隻胡人的駿馬回來，大家都祝賀他。他卻說："可能是禍呢？"他的兒子喜歡騎馬，一天從馬上跌下摔斷了腳。大家又慰問他，這位父親卻說："可能是福呢？"過了一年，胡人入侵，男子壯健的都要參戰，大部份不是死便是傷，只有他的兒子因為摔斷了腿，父子得以保全性命。所以，這個故事教訓我們：福可變為禍，禍可變為福！

A good professor has to retire because he is 65 years old. Some friends comment that it may be a blessing in disguise as the professor will be able to teach part time at various institutions, so more students from other institutions will be able to learn from the professor! (一位很好的教授因為已 65 歲,所以要退休了。一些朋友評論說:"禍福倚伏,可能是福呢!"教授現在於幾間不同的大專院校兼教,因而更多學生可以向那位教授學習!)

A bolt from the blue
晴天霹靂

Out of the blue / Out of a clear blue sky / 平地風波 / 無風起浪 / 風雲突變 / 不測風雲

此英文成語的意思,是突然發生一些令人感到驚訝,措手不及的事情,好像晴空突然出現一道閃電。中文也有類似成語,如晴天霹靂,好像晴空突然打雷,發生一些令人震驚的事情 / 景象。

巴金《懷念蕭珊》三:"真是晴天霹靂!我和我女兒,女婿趕到醫院,她那張病床上連床墊也給拿走了。"

冰心《老舍和孩子們》:"這對我是一聲晴天霹靂,這麼一個充滿了活力的人,怎麼會死呢?"

西方十九世紀思想家 Thomas Carlyle 亦曾在他的書 *The French Revolution* (1837) 有類似的句子:"Arrestment, sudden really as a bolt out of the blue, has hit strange victims."

On June 6, 1944, the Allies landed on Normandy and defeated the German armies. It was **a bolt from the blue** to Adolf Hitler! (1944 年 6 月 6 日，盟軍登陸諾曼第並擊敗德軍，對希特拉而言，真是晴天霹靂！)

A burned child dreads the fire
驚弓之鳥

Once bitten, twice shy / 一朝被灼燒，三年怕火光 / 一朝被蛇咬，三年怕草繩 / 心有餘悸

此英文成語的意思是若一個人曾經遭遇挫敗或者一些負面經歷，會令他因不想再受傷害而避免類似的環境或情況。

參看
REFERENCE

《穀梁傳・成二年疏》：「敗軍之將不可以語勇，驚弦之鳥不可以應弓。」

例子
EXAMPLES

John was almost drowned in a shipwreck when he was a child. Perhaps "**a burnt child dreads the fire**." John is afraid of water, the sea and the ocean now. （約翰年少時曾遇沉船，險遭溺斃，可能是驚弓之鳥吧，他現在很怕水和海洋。）

A drop in the bucket
杯水車薪

A drop in the ocean / 九牛一毛 / 滄海一粟 / 微不足道 / 於事無補

此英文成語的意思是力量很微薄，如一大桶水裏的一滴水，對於解決問題沒有太大作用，中文也有類似成語，如杯水車薪，用一杯水去救一車燃燒的木柴，比喻力量太小，沒有幫助。

參看 REFERENCE

The Bible, Old Testament, Isaiah (40:15): "Behold, the nations are as a drop of a bucket, and are counted as the small dust of the balance: behold, he taketh [take] up the isles as a very little thing." (《聖經‧舊約》，《以賽亞書》(40:15)：「看哪，萬民都像水桶的一滴，又算如天秤上的微塵：看哪，他舉起眾海島、好像極微之物。」)

《孟子告子上》：「今之為仁者，猶以一杯水，救一車薪之火也，不熄，則謂之水不勝火。」

The Edinburgh Weekly Journal, (July 1802): "The votes for the appointment of Bonaparte to be Chief Consul for life are like **a drop in the ocean** compared with the aggregate of the population of France."

例子 EXAMPLES

That company lost tremendously in the Financial Tsunami. Even though some colleagues were willing to donate half of their salaries to the company, that would be only **a drop in the bucket**. Finally, the CEO made the painful decision to shut down the company. (該公司在金融海嘯受到重創。儘管一些同事願意捐半薪給公司，但那只是杯水車薪，最後，總裁只好作出痛苦的決定 — 關閉公司。)

A flash in the pan
曇花一現

此英文成語可能來自十九世紀美國加州的尋金熱。當尋金者看到一些閃爍的光時，往往希望見到的是金，不過，當他們發現不是金的時候，只好慨歎不過是 **a flash in the pan.**。中文也有類似的成語，如曇花一現，指事物轉瞬即逝。

✦ 參看
REFERENCE

Paul Haworth, *Trailmakers of the Northwest* (1921): "The Colonel had told them that a cubic foot of gravel would pan out twenty dollars in gold."

你知道嗎
DO YOU KNOW?

曇花只開花一段短時間，有時只開一個晚上，到了第二天花便會凋謝。

A friend in need is a friend indeed
患難見真情

A fair-weather friend

此英文成語的意思是遇到艱難困境時，才知道誰是真正的朋友。與它意義相反的有 Where were you when I needed you most? 及 You left me when I needed you most.。著名歌手 Randy VanWarmer 的一首愛情流行曲 "Just When I Needed You Most" 裏，就有這句反義的用語：

"Just When I Needed You Most"

You packed in the morning,'

Cause you **left me just when I needed you most**

Left me just when I needed you most ...

Quintus Ennius (3rd century B.C.): *"Amicus certus in re incerta cernitur."* (Latin) 意思是:"當遇到困難時,你便知道誰是真朋友。" ("a sure friend is known when in difficulty.")

Caxton's *Sonnes of Aymon* (1489): "It is sayd [said], that at the nede [need] the frende [friend] is knowen [known]."

The morality play *Everyman* (late 15th century) 亦有類似的句子:"Fellowship: Sir, I say as I will do in deed. Everyman: Then be you a good friend at need."

A 你知道嗎
DO YOU KNOW?

《伊索寓言》裏有一個 "熊和兩個旅行者" 的故事 (*Aesop's Fables*, "The Bear and the Two Travellers"):兩個朋友在森林散步,其中一個突然看見有一隻熊走近,他立刻爬上樹 (沒有通知他的朋友),另一人見到熊時已太遲,只好倒在地上暫停呼吸,假裝死亡 (據說熊不吃死人的),熊在那人的鼻嗅着,覺得那人好像沒有呼吸,便走了。樹上的人爬下來後,好奇地問:"熊在你的臉上嗅着,好像和你說話,牠說了甚麼呢?" 另一人諷刺地答道:"熊對我說:'A friend in need is a friend indeed' — 即是你不是真朋友!(* 但現在卻普遍譯成 "患難見真情"?!)

A little learning / knowledge is a dangerous thing
一知半解

此英文成語的意思是只掌握膚淺學問的人,但他卻覺得自己無所不知,是最危險的。中文也有類似的成語,如一知半解,俗語就是 "知少少,扮代表"。

✶ 參看
REFERENCE

Alexander Pope (1688-1744), *An Essay on Criticism* (1709): "**A little learning is a dangerous thing**; drink deep, or taste not the Pierian spring: there shallow draughts intoxicate the brain, and drinking largely sobers us again."

The Monthly Miscellany; or Gentleman and Lady's Complete Magazine, Vol. II, (1774): "Mr. Pope says, very truly, **A little knowledge is a dangerous thing**."

A man of many parts
多才多藝

Have more than one string to one's bow / A man of all-roundedness / A Renaissance man

此英文成語的意思,是指一個人擁有多方面的才華和技能。中文也有類似成語,如多才多藝。

✶ 參看
REFERENCE

《南史．梁紀下．敬帝》:"高祖固天攸縱,聰明稽古,道亞生知,學爲博物,允文允武,多藝多才。"

例子
EXAMPLES

Leonardo da Vinci was not only gifted and talented in painting and sculpture, he was also good at anatomy. He is **a man of many parts (a man of all-roundedness)**. Indeed, he is really **a Renaissance man**! (達文西不但精於繪畫及雕塑,他亦專於解剖學,他真是一個多才多藝的文藝復興人!)

A penny pincher
一毛不拔

斤斤計較 / A mean miser

此英文成語的意思是形容一個人極其吝嗇。中文也有類似成語，如一毛不拔。

參看
REFERENCE

Thomas Dekker's play *Shomakers* [*Shoemakers*] *Holiday*, (1600): "Let wine be plentiful as beere [beer], and beere [beer] as water, hang these penny pinching fathers."

你知道嗎
DO YOU KNOW?

春秋戰國時代，有一位哲學家名叫楊朱 — 他主張"貴己"、"為我"，並提倡"個人自我中心"主義，遭孟子批評："拔一毛以利天下而不為"，因而有"一毛不拔"這句成語。

例子
EXAMPLES

Even though that millionaire is rich, he is a mean miser and he never donates a dollar to help the poor and needy. He is indeed **a penny pincher**. （雖然那個百萬富翁很有錢，不過他很吝嗇 — 他從不幫助那些貧困的窮人。他真是一個一毛不拔的孤寒財主。）

A rolling stone gathers no moss
滾石不生苔

轉業不聚財

此英文成語裏的"滾石"，是指流浪的人，不安於一個地方或一份工作，這樣難以做出成績或有所成就，因而有不可靠的意思。

参看
REFERENCE

Erasmus (in the third volume of his collection of Latin proverbs), *Adagia* (1508).

John Heywood, *A Dialogue Conteinyng the Nomber in Effect of All the Prouerbes in the Englishe Tongue* [*A Dialogue Containing the Number in Effect of All the Proverbs in the English Tongue*] (1546): "The rollyng [rolling] stone neuer [never] gatherth [gathers] mosse [moss]."

A stab in the back
背後插刀

A secret arrow injures a man (暗箭傷人) / Hit below the belt 刀刺在背

此英文成語的意思，是被人在背後陷害 (暗算)，通常是被自己所信任的人所害。

第一次世界大戰，德國戰敗，不少德國民族主義者譴責外國人與非民族主義者向德國 "背後插刀" (德語是 *Die Dolchstoßlegende* (German))，出賣德國。

1933 年，納粹在德國掌權，他們亦指 1920 年代的威瑪共和 (Weimar Republic) 向國家 "背後插刀" — 出賣德國。

例子
EXAMPLES

One of the most popular themes in movies and TV series has been about power politics in office – about **stabbing in the back** against each other among colleagues. (電影和電視劇集最流行的題材之一是辦公室內的權力鬥爭 — 員工之間互相背後插刀 / 暗箭傷人。)

11

A stitch in time saves nine
及時縫一針，將來省九針

小洞不補，大洞難補

此英文成語的意思，是若能即時解決問題，就可以節省時間和功夫。

參看
REFERENCE

Thomas Fuller's *Gnomologia, Adagies and Proverbs, Wise Sentences and Witty Sayings, Ancient and Modern, Foreign and British.* (1732): "**A stitch in time may save nine.**"

Better late than never（亡羊補牢，未為晚也）

例子
EXAMPLES

The teacher always reminds the students to study everyday, not to wait until the last minute before the examination – "**a stitch in time saves nine!**"（老師經常提醒學生要每天溫習，不要等考試前的最後一分鐘才臨急抱佛腳 — 及時縫一針，將來省九針啊！）

A white elephant
大白象

大而無當

此英文成語的意思是擁有沒用但極昂貴或難以照顧的事物，會惹來很大麻煩。

在泰國，白象是神聖的。不過，養一隻白象十分昂貴，所以，若泰王不喜歡一個人，會送他一隻白象 — 這樣可能會令那人破產。

▽ 參看
REFERENCE
G. E. Jewbury's *Letters* (1892): "His services are like so many **white elephants**, of which nobody can make use, and yet that drain one's gratitude, if indeed one does not feel bankrupt."

All he touches turns to gold
點石成金

The Midas touch / The golden touch

此英文成語的意思，是指一個人做任何事都很容易成功，來自希臘神話，是 Midas 的神話中最有名的的故事：據說，有一次，酒神狄俄倪索斯 (Dionysus) 發現他的老師西勒諾斯不見了。原來西勒諾斯醉酒之後到處亂跑，被一些農民捉住了。農民將西勒諾斯帶到國王彌達斯 (King Midas) 那裏。Midas 因為參加過酒神節，立刻認出了西勒諾斯。他趕緊釋放了西勒諾斯，並款待他十日十夜，之後把他交還給 Dionysus。其他版本的神話則說 Midas 是設計灌醉西勒諾斯並捉住他。總之，Midas 把自己手裏的西勒諾斯送回 Dionysus 處，而酒神 Dionysus 為了報答 Midas，承諾給予 Midas 他想要的任何東西。Midas 表示希望擁有點石成金的技能。Dionysus 答應了，於是 Midas 得到了點金術 — 凡是他接觸的東西都會變成金子。

中國成語也有點石成金，意思是修飾詩詞文章，使其生色不少。

✶ 參看
REFERENCE
（宋）胡元任《苕溪漁隱叢話後集‧孟浩然》："詩句以一字為工，自然穎異不凡，如靈丹一粒，點石成金也。"

美國加州大學 (University of California) 於 1980 年代，曾有巨額盈餘，一度推出 "golden handshake" 計劃 — 以巨額款項利誘老教授退休 (美國沒有退休年齡，老教授原則上可以不退休。) 。

All that glitters is not gold
閃爍光芒的未必是金

Judge not according to the appearance / You cannot know wine by the barrel / All cats are grey in the dark / Beauty is but skin-deep / A fair face may be a foul bargain / There is no trusting appearance (不可以貌取人) / 表裏不一 / 人不可以貌相 / 金玉其外，敗絮其中 (Gold and jade outside, but corrupted inside) / 以貌取人 / 失之子羽

此英文成語的意思是外表美好的事物，實際上未必如外表看來那麼好。中文也有類似的成語，如金玉其外，敗絮其中。故事來自明代劉基 (伯溫)《賣柑者言》：杭州有個賣水果的人，他賣的柑表面很光亮新鮮，如金的耀眼，如玉的潤澤，但買回家後才發覺柑的內裏乾得像破棉絮！當被質問時，賣柑者笑着答道："世界上很多東西、事物都往往是 '金玉其外，敗絮其中' 的"。作者藉賣柑者之口，諷刺社會腐敗，一些表面風光又居高位的達官貴人，只不過是 "金玉其外，敗絮其中"，虛有其表的庸才。

孔子的一個弟子子羽，是魯國人，子羽的相貌很醜陋，本來想跟隨孔子，孔子卻覺得他相貌醜陋，因而認為他資質低劣，不會成才。但子羽努力學習，致力修身實踐，處事光明正大。後來，子羽遊歷到長江，跟隨他的弟子有三百多人，聲譽很高，大家都傳誦他的名字。孔子聽說了這件事，感慨地說："… 之

前我只憑相貌便去判斷子羽的能力，結果對子羽的判斷就錯了！"（來自《史記·仲尼弟子列傳》："吾以言取人，失之宰之；以貌取人，失之子羽。"）

All roads lead to Rome
條條大路通羅馬

There are more ways to the wood than one / Follow the river and you will get to the sea / 殊途同歸 / 百川歸海

此英文成語 All roads lead to Rome（條條大路通羅馬）的出現，是因為古羅馬的道路，都是由首都羅馬如車輪軸一般向四方散開。中文也有類似的成語，如殊途同歸，意思是用不同的方法達至相同的結果。

參看
REFERENCE

《易經·繫辭下》："天下同歸而殊塗，一致而百慮。"
孫中山《中國問題的真解決》："這三種人殊途同歸，終將以日益增大的威力與速度，達到預期的結果。"

你知道嗎
DO YOU KNOW?

古羅馬人建築了由各地通往首都羅馬的道路網，因而有"條條大路通羅馬"，現在亦有殊途同歸的意思。

例子
EXAMPLES

Most people think that there is only one way to success – to work in the popular kinds of work. Actually, if we work hard, there are many other roads to success – "**all roads lead to Rome**!"（很多人以為只有從事受歡迎或熱門的工作才是成功之道。其實，只要我們努力，這個世界有很多其他行業、途徑，可以帶領我們成功，正所謂行行出狀元 — 即是"條條大路通羅馬！"）

An eye for an eye, a tooth for a tooth
以牙還牙，以眼還眼

Pay one back with his own coin

此英文成語的意思是指得到相稱的懲罰，可以追溯至古代
美索畢達米亞 (Mesopotamia)，巴比倫帝王 Hammurabi
(*c*. 1792 to 1750 B.C.) 的法典 *Code of Hammurabi* (*c*. 1754
B.C.)。

參看 REFERENCE

The Bible, New Testament, Matthew (5:38)："Ye [You] have heard
that it hath [has] been said, **An eye for an eye, and a tooth for a
tooth.**" (《聖經‧新約》,《馬太福音》(5:38)："你們聽見有話說：
'以眼還眼，以牙還牙。'")

例子 EXAMPLES

"**An eye for an eye, a tooth for a tooth**" sounds primitive and
cruel. However, in ancient times, the rich and powerful people could
hurt others and get away from punishment. So, King Hammurabi
of Babylon would like to make it fair for all free citizens, and thus,
having this law included in his *Code of Hammurabi.* ("以牙還牙，
以眼還眼" 看似原始又殘酷，不過，古代時，有財有勢的人往往
傷人而不受處分，所以，巴比倫帝王 Hammurabi 希望所有自由
民都得到平等待遇，因而把 "以牙還牙，以眼還眼" 納入他的法
典。)

As wise as Solomon
聰明如所羅門王　聰明智王

此英文成語的意思是聰明如所羅門王，即是聰明絕頂。

King Solomon（所羅門王，源自希伯萊文），是《舊約聖經》中的智慧君王，他最著名的故事是判斷誰是嬰孩的親生母親：故事是兩名婦人爭着認自己是一個嬰孩的親母，有智慧的 Solomon 裝作要把嬰孩劈成兩半，假母親不反對，真母親卻哭着哀求，寧願不要孩子也不願意傷害嬰孩，結果 Solomon 憑智慧找到誰是嬰孩的親生母親。另有一次，示巴王后（Queen Sheba）做了一些假花，幾可亂真，她把這些假花放在真花旁，問所羅門王能否不觸摸它們而分辨出兩者，於是聰明的所羅門王打開窗，看見蜜蜂飛往真花，遂成功分辨出真花和假花。

> **你知道嗎**
> **DO YOU KNOW?**
> 到了現在，Solomon 已成為智者的同義詞。
>
> **As wise as Solomon** 就是稱讚一個人有智慧的成語。⇄

At sixes and sevens
七上八下

心亂如麻 / 心煩意亂 / 亂七八糟 / 手足無措

此英文成語的意思，是指一種混亂的狀態，最早可見於 Geoffrey Chaucer, *Troilus and Criseyde* (1374): "Lat [Let] nat [not] this wrechched [wretched] wo [woe] thyn [your] herte [heart] gnawe [gnaw], but manly set the world on sexe and seuene [sixes and sevens]."

著名的百老匯歌劇 "貝隆夫人" 之主題曲 (the theme song of the Broadway Musical, Evita) **"Don't Cry for Me Argentina"** 亦有這句：

"Don't Cry for Me Argentina"

It won't be easy, you'll think it strange
When I try to explain how I feel

…

Although she's dressed up to the nines
At sixes and sevens with you

…

* (CHORUS) Don't cry for me Argentina
The truth is I never left you

…

參看 REFERENCE

Leti, *Il Cardinalismo di Santa Chiesa*, (1670): "They leave things at sixes and sevens."

Be made for each other
天生一對

Two of the same kind / Two of a kind

此英文成語的意思是指一對戀人在各方面都很合襯，像是上天所賜的一對絕配情侶。

你知道嗎
DO YOU KNOW?
曾經有一齣荷里活歌舞電影，由 Olivia Newton-John 和 John Travolta 主演，電影名字就是 "Two of a Kind" 天生一對！

例子
EXAMPLES
Peter and Mary are handsome, pretty, gifted and talented, so everyone praises them in their wedding party that they are **made for each other.** （彼得英俊，瑪麗漂亮，兩人資優又天才橫溢，所以，在他們的婚宴中，大家都讚他倆是天生一對。）

Be of one voice
異口同聲

此英文成語的意思是不同的人對某人或某事具有一致的看法。

參看
REFERENCE
《初刻拍案驚奇》卷二十：「眾人異口同聲，讚歎劉公盛德。」

你知道嗎
DO YOU KNOW?
本書附錄六參考書目 (Appendix VI References) 有一本書的中英文名字正是：《異口同聲 Be of One Voice: 中英成語 800 對 (修訂版)》陳永禎、陳善慈編著 (香港：商務，2011)。

Beauty in the eyes of the beholder
情人眼裏出西施

此英文成語的意思是美麗是主觀的 (The perception of beauty is subjective)，來自莎士比亞名劇《愛的徒勞》(William Shakespeare, 1564-1616, *Love's Labours Lost* (1588)): "Good Lord Boyet, my beauty, though but mean, Needs not the painted flourish of your praise; Beauty is bought by judgement of the eye, Not utter'd by base sale of chapmen's tongues."

參看 REFERENCE

David Hume's Essays, Moral and Political (1742): "Beauty in things exists merely in the mind which contemplates them."

你知道嗎 DO YOU KNOW?

春秋時代，越國有一位美女，名叫西施 (她被譽為中國四大古典美人之一)。據說西施在溪邊浣紗時，魚兒見到西施的美貌都自愧不如，羞慚到沉到水底，另一說是魚兒見到西施的美貌都為之傾倒而沉下水底。後來越國被吳國所滅，越王勾踐忍辱負重，一方面臥薪嘗膽，激勵自己；另一方面，他想用美人計迷惑吳王夫差，越國臣子范蠡找到西施，獻給吳王夫差，令夫差因而荒廢朝政，最終亡國。

又，"沉魚落雁之容，閉月羞花之貌" 都是形容女子的美貌。

Beauty is but skin-deep

★ 參看
REFERENCE
本書正文的 All that glisters is not gold

Better late than never
亡羊補牢（未為晚也）

遲到總比不到好 / 遲做總比不做好 / 晚來總比不來好

Geoffrey Chaucer 似乎是西方最早使用這句成語的，請參看 "The Yeoman's Prologue and Tale", *Canterbury Tales* (1386): "For better than never is late; never to succeed would be too long a period." 其他版本："For bet [better] than never is late."

你知道嗎
DO YOU KNOW?

《戰國策·楚策》："見兔而顧犬，未為晚也；亡羊而補牢，未為遲也。"

戰國時代，楚國有位大臣名莊辛，他向楚襄王勸諫，不要貪圖享樂，否則楚國會亡。楚王不信，莊辛於是避居趙國。果然，數月後，秦國入侵，大敗楚國。楚襄王想起並請教莊辛，莊辛道："亡羊補牢，未為遲也。"（意思是：羊走失了才去修補圍欄，這樣做還不算太遲。）終於楚王重用莊辛，收復了部份失地。

例子
EXAMPLES

Tommy did poorly in the mid-term test, but his teacher encourages him that if he works harder, he may pass his final examination with

flying colours – it is still not too late and **"better late than never**!"
（湯美在中期測驗考得很差，不過，他的老師鼓勵他：若他努力溫習，仍未太遲，他可以在期終考試考得好成績 —"亡羊補牢，未為晚也！"）

Between the devil and the deep blue sea
進退兩難

In a dilemma / 騎虎難下 / 騎上虎背

此英文成語的意思是面對艱難的環境，很難作出相應的行動，無論是進或退，也不容易作出正確的選擇。

參看
REFERENCE

Robert Monro's *His Expedition with the Worthy Scots Regiment (Called Mac-keyes Regiment).* (1637): "I, with my partie [party], did lie on our poste [post], as betwixt [between] the devill [devil] and the deep sea."

你知道嗎
DO YOU KNOW?

據說老虎的眼只能直視，不能看到自己的背，所以，當人騎上虎背時可以說是安全的，相對而言，若那人從虎背下來，反為危險，因為老虎會看見那人。

《伊索寓言》裏有一個"小鹿與洞中的獅子"的故事 (*Aesop's Fables*, "The Hind [Young deer] and the Lion in a Cave")：有一隻小鹿被獵人追捕，牠逃進一個山洞，卻發現原來是獅子洞，當獅子要吃他時，他哭着說："我原本以為逃過一劫，卻走進另一更大的劫！"這個寓言教訓我們：人類有時因害怕一些小危險而落入更大的危險之中。(Men, fearing a lesser danger, sometimes throw themselves into a greater one.)

我們又可以參看希臘神話 ─ 荷馬《奧德賽》(Homer's Odyssey, Greek mythology): "being caught between the devil and the [deep blue] sea" – Odysseus was being caught between Scylla [a six-headed monster] and Charybdis [a whirlpool].

Beyond one's grasp
鞭長莫及

Reach exceeds his grasp / Out of reach / 遠水不能救近火

《左傳・宣公十五年》："伯宗曰：不可。古人有言曰：可雖鞭之長，不及馬腹。'及天方授楚，未可與爭，雖晉之強，能違天乎？"（春秋時代，楚國攻打宋國，宋國向晉國求救，晉景公本想援助宋國，但被大臣伯宗勸止："大王不要啊！古語有云：'雖鞭之長，不及馬腹。'要知道楚國好比馬肚子，並不是鞭子可到的地方。現在楚國稱雄，是上天賜的，我們不適宜和楚國對抗。我國雖強，難道可以違抗天命嗎？'"）

Blood is thicker than water
血濃於水

✦ 參看
REFERENCE
Walter Scott (1771-1832), *Guy Mannering*, (1815): "Weel [Well], blude's [blood's] thicker than water; she's welcome to the cheeses and the hams just the same."

⚘ 例子
EXAMPLES
Chinese in Hong Kong, Macau, Taiwan and mainland China are from the same ancestors, **"blood is thicker than water"**, of course,

we should unite together. (香港、澳門、台灣和中國的中國人是同祖、同種、同源，"血濃於水"，當然我們要團結一起。)

Blow hot and cold
三心兩意

mercurial (善變)

你知道嗎
DO YOU KNOW?

化學元素水銀 (mercury) 極不穩定，(太陽系最近太陽的行星：水星 "Mercury" 亦是自轉和公轉都很快的)，所以，英文形容詞 "mercurial" 是善變的意思。

例子
EXAMPLES

Yesterday, John wanted to watch movie A. This morning, he changes his mind and suggested watching movie B. But now, he changes his mind again and asks us to go to watch movie C with him. Oh! John is so mercurial – he blows hot and cold all the time! (昨天，約翰說想看甲電影，今早他改變主意而建議看乙電影，不過現在他又再改變主意而要求我們陪他看丙電影。約翰真善變 "**mercurial**" — 他常常三心兩意 "**blow hot and cold**"！)

Burn one's boats / bridge
破釜沉舟

burn one's boats 是 "破釜沉舟" 的意思。這句成語與古羅馬軍隊有關。相傳古羅馬凱撒 (Julius Caesar) 等名將,在進攻敵方之前,會燒掉自己的軍船 (burn one's boats),藉此向士兵表示後路已斷,只能拼死奮勇向前。

中國也有類似的歷史故事。秦末,陳勝、吳廣起義,當時,秦將章邯帶領大軍包圍趙地巨鹿,楚地起義軍領袖派將軍宋義和副將項羽率兵救援,但宋義因害怕秦軍而按兵不動。項羽見士兵都願意作戰,便殺了宋義,指揮軍隊渡河,當部隊到了彼岸,便下令鑿沉所有渡河的船隻,並砸碎所有做飯用的鍋子(釜),表示誓死一戰的決心。之後,項羽的軍隊和秦兵決戰,楚軍最後大勝。(《史記‧項羽本紀》)

你知道嗎 DO YOU KNOW?

古羅馬軍隊除了燒掉自己的戰船以表示決心之外,也會過河燒橋 (burn one's bridges),目的和燒船一樣,都是想士兵知道自己無路可退,只能拼命奮勇向前作戰。

例子 EXAMPLES

Peter would like to take up a job offer at a new company in Macau, but, on the other hand, he does not want to burn his boats with that company. (彼得覺得澳門新公司那份工作頗具吸引力,但另一方面,他又不想因那間公司而斷絕了自己的後路。)

By hook and by crook
(By whatever means necessary – be they fair or foul)
千方百計

用盡方法

此英文成語的意思是用盡不同的方法（千方百計）去達到目的。

參看
REFERENCE

John Gower, *Confessio Amantis*, (1390): "What with hepe [hook] and what with croke [crook] they make her maister [master] ofte [often] winne [delight]."

Philip Stubbes, *The Anatomie of Abuses* (1583): "Either by hooke [hook] or crooke [crook], by night or day."

例子
EXAMPLES

Donald Trump, **by hook and by crook**, has been trying to make America strong again, whether it is true or not, at least that is what he thinks anyway. （特朗普千方百計嘗試令美國再次強大起來，是否真的如此 — 至少這是他自以為是的想法。）

Can't help falling in love
情不自禁

此成語表示不由自主,控制不住自己。

美國流行曲巨星 Elvis Presley 曾有一首很受歡迎的名曲,亦叫 **"Can't Help Falling in Love"**:

"Can't Help Falling in Love"

Wise men say only fools rush in

But I can't help falling in love with you

Shall I stay

Would it be a sin

If I can't help falling in love with you

參看
REFERENCE

《紅樓夢》第十五回:"寶玉情不自禁,然身在車上,只得眼角留情而已。"

Carpe Diem (Latin)
Seize the day
(Enjoy the moment)
把握現在　活在當下

這句來自古羅馬詩人賀拉斯的詩 (Horace, 65-8 B.C., *Odes*):Seize the day, trusting as little as possible in the future(即是"活在當下,別輕信未來,因為未來無法預知,所以我們應該把握現在!")

參看
REFERENCE
詩人賀拉斯也有類似的名句："**Seize the day**, and put the least possible trust in tomorrow."

你知道嗎
DO YOU KNOW?

1989 年的電影 "暴雨驕陽"（"Dead Poets Society"）亦曾經引用這句，當年美國電影協會更選這句為 "百大電影經典對白之一！"

Cast pearls before swine
對牛彈琴

此英文成語的意思是把珍貴之物、意念或建議送給不會欣賞的人。以下是類似的句子：*The Bible, New Testament, Matthew* (7:6) "Do not give what is holy to the dogs; nor cast your pearls before swine, lest they trample them under their feet, and turn and tear you in pieces." （《聖經·新約》,《馬太福音》(7:6)："不要把聖物給狗，也不要把你們的珍珠丟在豬面前，否則他們會踐踏珍珠，並轉過來咬你們。"）

14 世紀作家 William Langland 在 *Piers Plowman*《農夫皮爾斯》也曾經使用這句成語："Noli mittere Margeri – perles Among hogges"

參看
REFERENCE
《弘明集》："公明儀為牛彈清角之操，伏食如故。非牛不聞，不合其耳矣。" 從前有個著名的音樂家公明儀，有一天他對着正在吃草的一頭牛彈了一曲 "清角之操"。牛沒有理會他，仍然低頭吃草。公明儀仔細觀察牛，覺得不是牛聽不到他的琴聲，而是聽不懂，於是他又彈了另一首像蚊子、牛蠅、小牛叫喚的樂曲，那頭牛立刻停止了吃草，搖尾豎耳聽起來。（漢·牟融《理惑論》）

例子
EXAMPLES

You are casting pearls before swine with your suggestions – Paul is as stubborn as an ox, he just will not listen. （你的建議等於對牛彈琴，保羅很固執，他是不會聽的。）

Caviar to the general
曲高和寡

陽春白雪知音少（寡）

這句來自莎士比亞 (William Shakespeare, 1564-1616) 的著名作品《哈姆雷特》(The Tragicall Historie of Hamlet, Prince of Denmarke (1599))，比喻懷才不遇，知音難求，也可以說是 A good thing unappreciated by the ignorant。

參看
REFERENCE

"Hamlet: I heard thee [you] speake [speak] me a speech once, but it was neuer [never] acted, or it was, not aboue [above] once, for the play I remember pleasd [pleased] not the million, t'was [it was] cauiary [caviary] to the general, ..."

你知道嗎
DO YOU KNOW?

春秋戰國時代，有一位大學者宋玉（是屈原的弟子），由於他的文章十分深奧難明，所以很少人懂得讚賞他，當楚王問很少人讚賞他的原因時，宋玉便用"曲高和寡"的故事來解釋：有一個人來到市集唱歌，最初唱通俗的歌謠，很多人會一起和唱，之後，他唱一些較高亢的輓歌，唱和的人便少了，又後來，當他唱深奧的"陽春白雪"，跟着唱和的人更少 — 因為曲調太高，能唱和的人自然少。

現在我們把能力越高，越少獲得別人欣賞的情況稱為"曲高和寡"。

Cogito Ergo Sum (Latin)
Je pense, donc je suis (French)
I think, therefore I am
我思故我在

這句來自法國哲學家笛卡兒 (Rene Descartes, 1596-1650), *Discourse on the Method*《方法論》(1637)。

著名的法國哲學家笛卡兒主張理性思考 — 指出我們要心存懷疑的思考分析，小心認真去求證事情的真確。

Come what (come) may
順其自然

這句來自莎士比亞 (William Shakespeare, 1564-1616) 的著名悲劇《馬克白》(*Macbeth*) (1603-1607), (I:3)：主角馬克白將軍遇見女巫，預言他會成為國王，馬克白回答道：若命運要他做國王，他就會順其自然去做國王，意思是：不管未來如何，一切順其自然吧！

著名歌手 Doris Day 所唱荷里活電影 "擒兇記" 的主題曲 "*Que Sera Sera* (French)" (Whatever will be will be)，裏面的歌詞亦有類似意思：

"Que Sera Sera **(French)"(Whatever will be will be)**

When I was just a little girl

I asked my mother, what will I be

Will I be pretty, will I be rich

Here's what she said to me.

…

(CHORUS) *Que Sera, Sera,*

Whatever will be, will be

The future's not ours, to see

Que Sera, Sera

What will be, will be.

…

⭐ 參看
REFERENCE

詩人維吉爾 (Virgil) 有一句名言：**"Come what may**, all bad fortune
is to be conquered by endurance."

⭐ 參看
REFERENCE

本書正文的 **Let it be**

Crying wolf (too often)
狼來了

失信於人 / 信用破產

這句的意思是在不需要別人幫忙的時候，發出虛假的警報，到日後真的需要援手時，別人以為是假的，都不會提供幫助。

★ 參看
REFERENCE

《伊索寓言》有一個 "狼來了" 的故事 (*Aesop's Fables*, "The Boy Who Cried Wolf")：從前，有一個牧羊小童在山上看顧羊羣。有一天，因為他太悶了，所以他向山下大叫 "狼來了"！來到大山下的大人便跑上山，卻發覺原來牧羊小童在說謊，如是這樣幾次之後，大家都不再相信這個牧羊小童了！後來，真的有狼來吃羊時，牧童又大叫 "狼來了"，但這次大家都不再相信牧童了！

這個寓言教訓我們不要說謊，因為將來即使說真話，人們也不會再相信，後悔已太遲了！(Liars will not be believed even when they tell the truth in the future!)

Damon and Pythias
刎頸之交

生死之交 / 患難之交 / 莫逆之交 (A sworn friend)

古希臘數學家 Pythagoras (*c.* 570-490 B.C.) 的兩個學生
Pythias 及 Damon 住在 Syracuse，他們是很好的朋友。後
來 Pythias 被當地的帝王 King Dionysius I (r. 405-367 B.C.)
控告謀反而判處死刑，Pythias 要求先回家處理一些事務，
好友 Damon 願作人質（若 Pythias 不回來，則願代他被處
死），結果，Pythias 雖遇上海盜而遲了返回，卻仍盡量趕回
挽救替他做人質的好友 Damon，帝王 Dionysius 得悉之後
深受感動，並釋放這對 "刎頸之交" 的好友，成為佳話！

參看 REFERENCE

刎頸之交《史記‧廉頗藺相如列傳》："卒相與歡，為刎頸之交。"
（中國戰國時代，藺相如立了大功，成為上卿，位於舊臣廉頗將
軍之上，廉頗十分憤怒，不斷侮辱藺相如，但藺相如則處處忍
讓廉頗，因為藺相如不想與廉頗自相殘殺。後來廉頗聽到原因，
十分慚愧，並往藺相如家跪地請罪，他們之後更成為 "刎頸之
交" 的好朋友！）

例子 EXAMPLES

General Lian Po (327-243 B.C.) and Prime Minister Lin Xiang Ru
were like **Damon and Pythias** – they were willing to sacrifice for
each other in friendship. （廉頗與藺相如是 "刎頸之交" 的好朋
友，他們可以為雙方友誼作出犧牲。）

Deeply regret (diplomatic term)
深表遺憾 (外交詞令)

這個外交詞令表面上看似很嚴重，但其實卻不是。

Professor Joachim Remak (美國加州大學歷史系教授) 在他的著作 *Origins of World War I* 指出：1914 年 第一次世界大戰爆發，英國與法國也應該負上一些責任，因為兩國最初只表示"深表遺憾"，這在外交詞令而言，即是不會參戰，因而誤導了德國，以為英法兩國不會開戰！(不過，後來，英法兩國卻參戰，導致第一次世界大戰爆發！)

你知道嗎 DO YOU KNOW?

1968 年，蘇聯入侵東歐捷克的布拉格 (Prague, Czechoslovakia), (鎮壓史稱 " 布拉格之春 ")，美國只是表示深表遺憾，這在外交詞令而言，即是不會開戰，結果亦真的沒有干預！(美國輿論界亦批評政府軟弱，並重刊盲眼小說家 James Thurber 的 "The Rabbits Who Caused All the Problems" (1939)，當年 James Thurber 批評納粹德國的侵略，今次輿論界則是暗批美國政府假仁假義，當真正面對極權國家，如納粹德國或蘇聯時，便無能為力！)

1962 年，古巴飛彈危機就不同了！President John F. Kennedy 不是用深表遺憾 / **deeply regret**，而是用 ultimatum (最後通牒) — 若不撤走飛彈便會開戰！幸好蘇聯及時撤走飛彈，因而解決了這次危機，避免了世界大戰。

2003 年，美國總統布殊 (President George W. Bush) 亦用 ultimatum (最後通牒) 警告伊拉克的薩達姆 · 侯賽因 (Saddam Hussein, Iraq)，而不是用"深表遺憾"，結果美國終於出兵入侵伊拉克！

Do in Rome as the Romans do
Si fueris Romae, Romano vivito more;
Si fueris alibi, vivito sicut ibi (Latin)
(When in Rome, do as the Romans do)
入鄉隨俗

此英文成語的意思是一個人到了異鄉或陌生的環境時,最好能夠跟隨當地的風俗習慣。

這是來自古羅馬帝國的米蘭主教聖安布羅斯 (St. Ambrose, bishop of Milan):

"Romanum venio, ieiuno Sabbato; hic sum, non ieiuno: sic etiam tu, ad quam forte ecclesiam veneris, eius morem serva, si cuiquam non vis esse scandalum nec quemquam tibi." ("When I go to Rome, I fast on Saturday, but here I do not. Do you also follow the custom of whatever church you attend, if you do not want to give or receive scandal.")

後來,聖奧古斯丁 (St. Augustine) 亦有引用聖安布羅斯這段說話。

例子
EXAMPLES

Paul used to like Chinese food in Hong Kong. But when he studied in California, he changed to love western food. When his friends laughed at him, he tried to explain, **"Do in Rome as the Romans do!"** (保羅在香港時喜歡中菜,但他往加州讀書時卻轉而喜愛西餐,當他的朋友嘲笑他時,他便解釋道,"入鄉隨俗" 嘛!)

Do not count your chickens before they are hatched

蛋還未孵，不要去計算小雞的數目

此英文成語的意思是若不肯定事情會如何發展下去時，就不要存有太多幻想，或者過早籌劃／夢想未來的大計。

《伊索寓言》有一個"擠牛奶的小姑娘"的故事 (*Aesop's Fables*, "The Milkmaid and Her Pail") :

一個擠牛奶的小姑娘，工作時只顧幻想將來 — 她幻想着：賣掉牛奶後，便去買雞生蛋，之後孵出很多小雞，賺了錢就可以買漂亮的裙子去參加舞會，之後很多男士追求她，不過，最後她卻不小心倒翻了牛奶桶！回到家，媽媽就用這句說話教訓她："蛋還未孵，不要去計算小雞的數目"即是工作未完成時，不要有太多幻想，否則只會空歡喜而終於甚麼都沒有！

Earn one's own bread
自食其力

Shift for oneself / Cut one's own grass / Paddle one's own canoe

此英文成語的意思是靠自己工作以維持生計。中文也有類似的成語，如自食其力。

參看
REFERENCE

(明) 方孝孺《企高軒記》："孺子業儒而太玄習道家言，孺子自食其力而太玄衣食于國。"(清) 蒲松齡《聊齋志異‧黃英》："自食其力不爲貪，販花爲業不爲俗。"(後漢) 佚名《太平經》：參看"各自衣食其力。"

例子
EXAMPLES

When Fred studied in California in the 1970s, most students from Hong Kong were hard working, and they **earned their own bread**. (於 1970 年代，張學明在加州讀書時，大部份的香港留學生都很用功，他們都是自食其力的。)

Every minute counts
分秒必爭 / 爭分奪秒

一刻千金 (seize the minute, seize the second) / 只爭朝夕 (seize the morning, seize the evening)

此英文成語的意思是把握時間，不容許浪費一分一秒。中文也有類似的成語，如分秒必爭。

參看
REFERENCE

(明) 徐復祚《投梭記‧卻說》："今朝寵命來首錫，掌樞衡只爭旦夕。"

毛澤東名句 "一萬年太久，只爭朝夕。"

〈滿江紅和郭沫若同志〉：

小小寰球，有幾個蒼蠅碰壁。

嗡嗡叫，幾聲淒厲，幾聲抽泣。

螞蟻緣槐誇大國，蚍蜉撼樹談何易。

正西風落葉下長安，飛鳴鏑。

多少事，從來急；

天地轉，光陰迫。

一萬年太久，只爭朝夕。

四海翻騰雲水怒，五洲震蕩風雷激。

要掃除一切害人蟲，全無敵。

Feathers of the same kind flock together

物以類聚，人以羣分

各從其類 / 同聲相應 / 同氣相求

此英文成語的意思是同類的人或事物通常聚集在一起，就好像同類型之羽毛的鳥會聚在一起。

參看
REFERENCE

西塞羅 Cicero, "Birds of a feather flock together."

《易經・繫辭上》："物以類聚，人以群分。"巴金《致〈十月〉》："好作品喜歡和好文章排列在一起，這也是所謂'物以類聚'吧。"

**你知道嗎
DO YOU KNOW?**

《易經・文言：乾》：上九日："亢龍有悔"。何謂也？"同聲相應，同氣相求。水流濕，火就燥，雲從龍，風從虎，聖人作而萬物覩。本乎天者親上，本乎地者親下，則各從其類也。"

**例子
EXAMPLES**

I believe that people get along with each other simply because they belong to the same kind – "**feathers of the same kind flock together.**"（人與人之間的相處，我很相信是物以類聚，人以羣分，所謂"人夾人緣"。）

Fortune favours the brave / bold
Fortuna audaces iuvat (Latin) (by Pliny the Elder, Rome)
Audentis Fortuna iuvat (Latin) (*Virgil, Aeneid*, Roman Empire)
天佑勇者

Luck is on the side of those who take chances / Luck favours the adventurous / 不入虎穴，焉得虎子 / 皇天不負有心人 / 天道酬勤 / 自助者天助 / 勇者無敵

此英文成語的意思是願意冒險的人往往可以取得成功。

你知道嗎 DO YOU KNOW?

Fortuna was the Roman goddess of Luck / Fortune. (Fortuna 是羅馬神話的幸運女神。)

Gather ye rosebuds while ye may
有花堪折直須折（莫待無花空折枝）

莫負好時光

這句的意思是勸人珍惜時光，來自 Robert Herrick (1591-
1674), "To the Virgins, to Make Much of Time":
Gather ye rosebuds while ye may,
Old Time is still a-flying;
And the same flower that smiles today,
Tomorrow will be dying.

含類似意思的中文歌詞如下："趁青春，結隊向前行"（新亞
書院校歌歌詞）
(唐)《金縷衣》作者：杜秋娘
勸君莫惜金縷衣，勸君惜取少年時。
花開堪折直須折，莫待無花空折枝。

參看
REFERENCE
本書正文的 *Carpe diem*（亦有類似的意思）

Give a man a fish, feed him for a day. Teach a man to fish, feed him for a lifetime.

授人以魚，不如授之以漁

這句的意思是若給人一條魚，只會給他一時的食物；但若教他釣魚的技能，他就可以靠自己捕魚的技能，長遠解決食物的問題。

參看
REFERENCE

《漢書‧董仲舒傳》："古人有言曰：'臨淵羨魚，不如退而結網。'"

你知道嗎
DO YOU KNOW?

現在的扶貧社會工作計劃都強調協助貧者自力更生，幫助他們有一技之長，才是長遠扶貧、滅貧之道。

Good appetite with bad teeth

眼高手低　志大才疏

To have great ambition but little talent / Aim high but accomplish little / Have grandiose aims but modest abilities./ One's goal is more than one can achieve / High ambition but no real ability

此英文成語的意思是一個人自視頗高，但能力卻低。

參看
REFERENCE

毛澤東《反對黨八股》："我勸這些同志先辦'少許'，再去辦'化'，不然，仍舊脫離不了教條主義和黨八股，這叫做眼高手低，志大才疏，沒有結果的。"

秦牧《藝海拾貝‧〈畫蛋‧練功〉》："比較成熟的藝術家，如果不是經常練功，欣賞的水平一天天高了，而表現的技術卻沒有相應提高，時長日久，就很容易形成'眼高手低'。"

你知道嗎
DO YOU KNOW?

德國的 Bismarck 下台後，一些年青將領有很多征服世界之大計，但他們卻沒有實力，即"眼高手低"，最終，德國於第一次世界大戰 (1914-1918) 戰敗。

例子
EXAMPLES

John is ambitious but with little talent. He has **good appetite with bad teeth**, thus, he seldom reaches his goal. （約翰野心勃勃，但卻沒有天份，可說是眼高手低 — 所以他很少達標。）

Gone with the wind
一去不返

此英文成語的意思是離開了就不再回頭，或是消失得無形無蹤，也可說成"一去不復回"。

參看
REFERENCE

Ernest Dowson, Cynara (1896)：

"I have forgot much, Cynara, **gone with the wind**".

你知道嗎
DO YOU KNOW?

荷里活亦有著名電影："**Gone with the Wind**"（有關美國南北戰爭的愛情故事），中文譯為"亂世佳人"（亦有譯作"飄"）。

Hide one's light under a bushel

深藏若虛

深藏不露 / 不露鋒芒 / 錦衣夜行

在古代，人點燈的原因，是要照亮四周，如果把點起的燈放在 "斗底下"(under a bushel)，就會失去其用處 (defeat its purpose)。以下是類似的句子：

The Bible, New Testament, Matthew (5:15)："Neither do men light a candle, and put it under a bushel, but on a candlestick; and it giveth [gives] light unto all that are in the house." (《聖經‧新約》,《馬太福音》(5:15)："人點燈，不放在斗底下，是放在燈臺上，就照亮一家的人。"

參看
REFERENCE
《史記‧老子韓非列傳》："吾聞之，良賈深藏若虛，君子盛德，容貌若愚。" 司馬貞索隱："深藏謂隱其寶貨，不令人見，故云 '若虛'。"

你知道嗎
DO YOU KNOW?
錦衣夜行來自《史記‧項羽本紀》："富貴不歸鄉，如衣錦夜行。" (項羽攻佔咸陽之後，有人勸他定都該地，但他卻思鄉而東歸，亦沒有稱皇帝，只稱楚霸王。)

If the mountain will not go to Muhammad, then Muhammad must go to the mountain
(If one's will does not prevail, one must submit to an alternative)

若大山不來，我就去大山

山不過來，我就過去

山不轉，路轉；路不轉，人轉

這句的意思是若未能實現自己的想法，便要退而求其次，作出另一個選擇，即是改變不了環境，就改變自己吧。

參看 REFERENCE
來自培根 (Francis Bacon), Essays (1625)："Mahomet [Muhammad] cald [call] the Hill to come to him. And when the Hill stood still, he was neuer [never] a whit abashed, but said; If the Hill will not come to Mahomet, Mahomet wil [will] go to the hil [hill]."

又 參看 REFERENCE
John Owen, (1643): "If the mountaine [mountain] will not come to Mahomet [Muhammad], Mahomet will goe [go] to the mountaine [mountain]."

In the Zone
得心應手

一帆風順 / 事事如意 / 心想事成 / 順風順水

此英文成語的意思是事情做起來非常順利。

It is better late than never

✳ 參看
REFERENCE
本書正文的 Better late than never

It seems like ages
一日不見，如隔三秋 / 一日三秋

望穿秋水 / 望眼欲穿

這句的意思是只是沒有見面一天，就覺得好像過了很長時間，通常用來形容情侶之間的思念。

✳ 參看
REFERENCE
《詩經》：

"彼采葛兮，一日不見，如三月兮。

彼采蕭兮，一日不見，如三秋兮。

彼采艾兮，一日不見，如三歲兮。"

📖 例子
EXAMPLES

Peter and Mary are lovers. But last year, Peter went to study in California for one year. They missed each other very much – to them, "**it seems like ages**!" (彼得和瑪麗是情人。但去年彼得去了加州進修一年，他們都很掛念對方 — 對他們來說真是 "一日不見，如隔三秋！")

Jack of all trades, master of none
博而不通，雜而不精

周身刀，冇張利（廣東話俗語）

此英文成語的意思是一個人可以做許多不同類型的工作，但卻沒有一種是他精通的。

參看
REFERENCE

The *Gentleman's Magazine* (1770):

"**Jack at all trades*,** is seldom good at any."

Charles Lucas, *Pharmacomastix*, (1785):

"The very Druggist, who in all other nations in Europe is but Pharmacopola [pharmacopoeia], a mere drug-merchant, is with us, not only a physician and chirurgeon [surgeon], but also a Galenic and Chemic apothecary; a seller of drugs, medicines, vertices, oils, paints or colours, poysons [poisons], etc. **a Jack of all trades**, and in truth, **master of none**."

例子
EXAMPLES

John is interested in many things, but he learns various things for only a short time and quits very soon – indeed, he is a "**Jack of all trades, master of none**." （約翰對很多事物都有興趣，但他對不同的東西只學習一段短時間便因失去興趣而放棄，他真是雜而不精。）

＊原文是用 at，現今多用 of。

Keep your chin up

挺起胸膛

類似的英文成語：Stand tall

此英文成語的意思是在困境裏仍然保持一份樂觀正面的態度，勉勵自己振作起來。

參看
REFERENCE

The Evening Democrat (October 1900), "Epigrams Upon the Health-giving Qualities of Mirth"): "**Keep your chin up**. Don't take your troubles to bed with you."

你知道嗎
DO YOU KNOW?

體操的運動員，（即使出錯或掉下來），最後的動作都是仰頭向上 "**keep their chins up**"！

例子
EXAMPLES

Professor Warren Hollister (1930-1997) was a world-renowned historian on medieval English history at the University of California, Santa Barbara. He had supervised 29 PhDs – all have been professors at various universities. Among the 29 PhDs, Dr. Fred Cheung was the only Chinese. One day, Fred asked Professor Hollister if he was the black sheep of the family. Professor Hollister answered, "No! Of course not! Frederick, you are really good, I am proud of you! **Keep your chin up**!" (Professor Hollister (1930-1997) 是加州大學著名的英國中古史教授，他指導過 29 位博士（全都是大學教授），但只有張學明（筆者）是中國人。有一天，筆者問師傅自己是否師門的害羣之馬 "black sheep of the family"？ Professor Hollister 回答道："當然不是！您真的很好，我以您為榮！挺起胸膛 "keep your chin up" 吧！")

Professor Hollister also taught Dr. Fred Cheung the beauty and the double meaning of the word, "appreciation" – to appreciate others and to be grateful. Learned scholars are always modest themselves, and they know how to appreciate others; so, we should be appreciative and grateful! (Professor Hollister 亦教導張學明博士學懂 "appreciation" 的雙重意思：欣賞及感恩 ─ 我們最重要是學會去 "欣賞" 別人，(越有學問的人越有胸襟去欣賞 / 賞識他人)，然後，我們亦要 "感恩" ！)

參看
REFERENCE

蘇軾 (東坡) 年少時，見到一個老和尚打坐，又學他打坐並問老和尚他像甚麼？老和尚答道："小施主，你像一尊佛在打坐。" 小東坡又問老和尚，知否自己像甚麼？老和尚答道："不知道。" 小東坡大笑說："像牛糞啊！"回家後，妹妹 (蘇小妹) 教導哥哥：老和尚的心境像佛，所以他看到甚麼都像佛，而哥哥你年少無知，所以才會覺得老和尚像牛糞。兩人的學識和修養，高下立見！(後來，蘇東坡長大了，學識和修養都變得有深度及成熟，他又信了佛並和很多高僧成為好朋友。)

Kick the bucket (slang 俚語)
死

Pass away / Die / 兩腳一伸

此英文俚語是非正式用語，解作 "死亡"，中文也有類似的詞彙，如 "拉柴"，或廣東話 "瓜左"。

荷里活電影："It's a Mad, Mad, Mad World"（瘋狂世界）就有一幕，一個男角死時，兩腳一伸，踢着一個水桶 ─ 相信是導演故意的安排，引來觀眾哄堂大笑！

Kill two birds with one stone / shaft

一石二鳥 / 一箭雙雕 / 一矢雙雕

一舉兩得

南北朝的北周宣帝時，有一位箭術高明的人，名長孫晟，後來他被派往突厥擔任外交使節。突厥王很欣賞長孫晟的箭術，有一天，突厥王與長孫晟狩獵時，看見天空中有兩隻雕在互爭一塊肉，突厥王請長孫晟射下兩隻雕，結果，長孫晟只射了一支箭便把兩隻雕一齊射下！大家都讚歎不已！

又 參看
REFERENCE

Thomas Hobbes, On Liberty (1656):

"to kill two birds with one stone, and satisfy two arguments with one answer." *Dictionary of Cliches* by James Rogers (New York: Facts on File Publications, 1985).

例子
EXAMPLES

This book not only enriches my knowledge in idioms (English, Chinese and translation), it has also enhanced my horizon in history and culture. Indeed, reading this book, I **"kill two birds with one stone!"** （這本書不但增加了我對成語（中英文及翻譯）之知識，更擴闊自己歷史文化之視野，研讀這本書真是"一石二鳥"（"一舉兩得"）！）

Kill the goose that lays the golden egg
殺雞取卵

意思是不要因貪心而因小失大。

《伊索寓言》裏有一個 "母雞生金蛋" 的故事，(*Aesop's Fables*, "The Hen that Laid Golden Eggs"):

一個人有一隻生金蛋的母雞，他以為那隻母雞的肚內有很多金蛋，遂剖開母雞的肚，卻發覺甚麼都沒有！

這個寓言教訓我們：應該滿足於自己所擁有的，不應貪心，否則，結果可能變得一無所有。

Let be gone be bygone
(Let the unpleasantness between us become a thing of the past)

既往不咎，忘掉舊嫌 / 過去的就讓它過去吧

Let sleeping dogs lie / Let all things past, pass

這句的意思是抱着一份放下的態度，忘記以往不愉快的經歷。

參看 REFERENCE

William Shakespeare, *The Winter's Tale* (1611):

"This satisfaction, the by-gone-day proclaym'd [proclaimed], say this to him."

一名蘇格蘭的教士 Samuel Rutherford 於 1636 寫的信，對自己年青時的愚昧感到歉咎，並向上主禱告：

"Pray that byegones [bygones] betwixt [between] me and my Lord may be byegones [bygones]."

例子 EXAMPLES

Tommy's girlfriend had left him, so he was very sad. But his teacher encouraged him to forget about the sad happenings and be strong again – "**let be gone be bygone**"！(湯美的女朋友離開了他，所以，他很傷心。不過他的老師鼓勵他忘記那些傷心往事，重新振作起來，"過去的就讓它過去吧！")

Let it be
順其自然

隨遇而安 / Let alone

此英文成語的意思是不執着，安然接受臨到自己身上的事情。

六十年代英國著名搖滾樂隊 The Beatles 有一首名曲就叫
"Let It Be"：

"Let It Be"

When I find myself in times of trouble

Mother Mary comes to me

Speaking words of wisdom, let it be.

Long and winding road
道阻且長 (《詩經》·《秦風》·《蒹葭》)

此英文成語的意思是路途漫長，困難重重，不容易繼續下去。

蒹葭蒼蒼，白露為霜。所謂伊人，在水一方。

溯洄從之，道阻且長。

溯游從之，宛在水中央。

六十年代英國著名搖滾樂隊 The Beatles 有一首流行名曲就
叫 **"The Long and Winding Road"**.

"The Long and Winding Road"

The long and winding road

That leads to your door

Will never disappear

I've seen that road before

...

Some experts believe that if China and the U.S.A. cooperate, both sides (and the world) will benefit. However, some scholars worry that the Sino-American relationship will be a **long and winding road**. （一些專家相信：若中國和美國合則兩利（甚至整個世界都得益），不過，一些學者擔心中美關係的前景是道阻且長。）

Look before you leap
Think twice (thrice) before you do anything
三思而行

此英文成語的意思是勸告我們要反覆考慮清楚後才付諸行動。

《伊索寓言》有一個 "狐狸與山羊" 的故事 (Aesop's Fables, "The Fox and the Goat")：

一隻掉進井的狐狸，見到有一隻山羊路過，便說井水很甜美，叫山羊跳下來，山羊立刻跳下井，卻給狐狸踏着背得以逃離那個井，臨走前，狐狸回頭對困在井裏的山羊說："下次跳下井前要'三思而後行'（思考清楚）啊！"

這個寓言教訓我們：做事要思考清楚，三思而後行，要計劃周詳才去做，不要未經思考就魯莽行事。

參看
REFERENCE

John Heywood, *A Dialogue Conteinyng the Number in Effect of All the Prouerbes in the Englishe Tongue* (1546) [*A Dialogue Containing the Number in Effect of All the Proverbs in the English Tongue*]:

"And though they seeme [seem] wives for you never so fit, Yet let not harmfull [harmful] haste so far out run your wit: ...

Thus by these lessons ye [you] may learne [learm] good cheape [bargain] / In wedding and all things to looke [look] ere [before] ye [you] leaped "**Look before you leap**"."

Look for a needle in a haystack
大海撈針

Trying to find a piece of straw in a haystack

此英文成語的意思是找到某人或某物的機會很渺茫，幾乎是無從尋覓。

參看
REFERENCE

Thomas More (1532): "To seek out one line in his books would be to go look for a needle in a meadow."

Miguel de Cervantes, *Don Quijote de la Mancha*, Book III: 10, (English translation): "As well look for a needle in a bottle [bundle] of hay."

又 參看
REFERENCE

《論語‧公冶長》："季文子三思而後行。子聞之，曰：'再，斯可矣。'"

(宋) 辛棄疾《哨遍》詞："嗟魚欲事遠遊時，請三思而行可矣。"

(元) 關漢卿《救風塵》第一摺："你也合三思而行，再思可矣。"

例子
EXAMPLES

The search for the missing Malaysian airplane in the Indian Ocean a few years ago was like "**looking for a needle in a haystack!**"（在印度洋尋找那消失的馬來西亞客機，如大海撈針，數年了，仍是音訊全無。）

Lose a ship for a halfpenny worth of tar
因小失大

Never spoil a ship for haporth of tar / 貪他一斗米，失掉半年糧

不要為了半分錢而損失一條船。Haporth 是英文口語，意思是 halfpenny worth（值半便士），即很少錢。船漏水，要塗柏油 (tar) 防漏，但為了節省少量的柏油，結果損失了整艘船，就是因小失大。（又傳說古英國諺語是 sheep 而不是 ship，因受傷的羊是用柏油塗治的，後來（十九世紀）英國航運發達，遂改 sheep 為 ship。）

參看
REFERENCE
《呂氏春秋》："達子請金齊王賞軍，齊王怒不給…及戰大敗…此貪於小利以失大利者也。"

你知道嗎
DO YOU KNOW?
日本也有類似的句子："惜一文而不知百事。"

Love at first sight
一見鍾情

Theia（忒亞），古希臘神話的 Titan（泰坦）巨神之一，是天神 Uranus（烏拉諾斯）和大地之母 Gaia（蓋亞）的女兒，象徵 "燦爛"。她和泰坦巨神族的 Hyperion（許珀里翁），生下太陽神 Helios（赫利俄斯）、月亮女神 Selene（塞勒涅）和黎明女神 Eos（厄俄斯）。原來 Theia 和古希臘哲學息息相關，Theia mania（即 divine madness 神賜的瘋狂），就是古希臘哲學家 Plato（柏拉圖）在 *Phaedrus* 的對話錄中，形

容人進入一種 divine madness 神聖瘋狂的狀況，通常用來
形容 "初戀或一見鍾情 (love at first sight) 的心理狀況"。

According to William Shakespeare's *Romeo and Juliet*, the two
youngsters fell in **love at first sight** (so romantic and touching). （根
據莎士比亞名劇《羅密歐與茱麗葉》，男女主角正是一見鍾情，
（十分浪漫感人）。）

Love me love my dog
(Love one's house and extend love to
the crows on the roof)
愛屋及烏

He that loves the tree loves the branch.

此英文成語的意思是因為愛某人而延伸至愛與此人有關的人。

參看
REFERENCE

《說苑・貴德》：

"太公對曰：'對臣聞愛其人者，兼屋上之烏；憎其人者，惡其
餘胥；餘胥烏者…' "

（姜太公答周武王："若喜愛一個人，亦會連帶愛他屋上的烏鴉；
若憎恨一個人，亦會連帶厭惡他的僕人；…"）

Make a mountain out of a molehill
小題大做

Storm in a teacup / Tempest in a teapot (US) (美式) / 茶杯裏的風波

據說公元二世紀，希臘有一個作家叫 Lucian（琉善），他寫的 "Ode to a Fly"《蒼蠅讚》，使用了 "to make an elephant of a fly"，即是 "把蒼蠅說成大象"，後來這句子亦成了法文和德文的成語。Make a mountain out of a mole hill，亦可見於 *Book of Martyrs* (1570)《殉道者名錄》。

> **參看**
> **REFERENCE**
> 《昭昧詹言》卷二十："〔山谷詩《雲濤石》〕全是以實形虛，小題大做，極遠大之勢，可謂奇想高妙。"
> 《紅樓夢》第七三回："沒有甚麼，左不過是他們小題大做罷了，何必問他？"
> 曹禺《雷雨》第四幕："〔魯貴〕覺得大海小題大做，煩惡地皺着眉毛。"

Make hay while the sun shines
未雨綢繆

防患未然 / 毋臨渴掘井，宜未雨綢繆

此英文成語的意思是勸告我們要預先做好準備工作。

> **參看**
> **REFERENCE**
> The Bible, Old Testament, Proverbs (10:5)："He that gathereth [gathers] in summer is a wise son: but he that sleepeth (sleeps) in harvest is a son that causeth [causes] shame." (《聖經 · 舊約》,《箴

言》(10:5)："夏天聚斂的，是智慧之子；收割時沉睡的，是貽羞之子。")

John Heywood, *A Dialogue Conteinyng the Nomber in Effect of All the Prouerbes in the Englishe Tongue* [*A Dialogue Containing the Number in Effect of All the Proverbs in the English Tongue*] (1546):

"Whan [When] the sunne [sun] shinth [shines] make hay. Whiche [Which] is to say. Take time whan [when] time cometh [comes], lest time steale [steal] away."

你知道嗎 DO YOU KNOW?

有一個在《詩經豳風：鴟鴞》裏的故事，講述在一場暴風雨裏，一隻鴟鴞母鳥失去了牠的小鳥，但牠仍努力築巢，以防備下一場風雨。又，《尚書·金滕篇》記載周公討伐管叔之後，作了〈鴟鴞〉的詩，內容是：趁着天還未下雨，用桑根的皮把鳥巢的空隙塞緊；只有堅固鳥巢，才可避免未來的風雨侵害。

例子 EXAMPLES

Even though the final examination is still three months from now, the teacher has reminded the students to study hard now – **to make hay while the sun shines** (and not to wait until the last minute).（儘管距離期終考試仍有三個月，老師已提醒同學現在要開始溫習，"毋臨渴掘井，宜未雨綢繆！"）

Man proposes and God disposes
Homo proponit, sed Deus disponit (Latin)
謀事在人，成事在天

這句的意思是事情由人籌劃，但成功與否，則在乎上天安排。

參看
REFERENCE

The Bible, Old Testament, Proverbs (16:9)："A man's heart deviseth [devises] his way: but the Lord directeth [directs] his steps." (《聖經·舊約》,《箴言》(16:9)："人心籌算自己的道路；惟上主指引他的腳步。")

The Bible, Old Testament, Proverbs (19:21)："There are many devices in a man's heart; nevertheless the counsel of the Lord, that shall stand." (《聖經·舊約》,《箴言》(19:21)："人心多有計謀；惟有上主的籌算才能立定。")

The Bible, Old Testament, Jeremiah (10:23)："O Lord, I know, that the way of a man is not in himself; it is not in man that walketh [walks] to direct his steps." (《聖經·舊約》,《耶利米書》(10:23)："主啊，我曉得人的道路不由自己，行路的人也不能定自己的腳步。")

Thomas Kempis, "Of the Limtation of Christ", Chapter 19 of Book 1: "For the resolutions of the just depend rather on the grace of God than on their own wisdom; and in Him they always put their trust, whatever they take in hand. **For man proposes, but God disposes**; neither is the way of man in his own hands".

你知道嗎
DO YOU KNOW?

Dominus (Latin) 即是 Lord，中文就是主、上主、天主。

Yahweh (Hebrew) 即是 Jehowah，中文是雅偉、耶和華。

My way
我行我素

Get one's (own) way

此英文成語的意思是按自己個人的喜好或意願行事。

著名經典流行曲 **"My Way"**(sung by Frank Sinatra, lyrics written by Paul Anka):

"My Way"

And now, the end is near

And so I face the final curtain

My friend, I'll say it clear

I'll state my case, of which I'm certain

I've lived a life that's full

I travelled each and every highway

And more, much more than this, I did it **my way**

…

The record shows I took the blows and did it **my way**!

Yes, it was **my way**!

例子
EXAMPLES

Frank Sinatra, the American singer and movie star, was famous for his style of acting and singing his own way, which could be reflected by his most popular song, "**My Way**."

美國歌影雙棲紅星法蘭仙納杜拉的風格是我行我素，而他最受歡迎的歌曲亦正是一首 "**My Way**"（我行我素）。

Necessity is the mother of invention
急中生智 / 需要乃發明之母

Hit upon an idea / In a flash of inspiration / 心生一計 / 情急智生

此英文成語來自《伊索寓言》"烏鴉和水罐" (Aesop's Fables, "The Crow and the Pitcher")，故事講述一隻烏鴉口渴想喝水罐中的水，可是喝不到，牠急中生智，把石子投入水罐裏面，終於喝到溢出來的水，而寓言的結尾就是這句話。

你知道嗎
DO YOU KNOW?
據說宋代的司馬光，年少時與小朋友在花園玩耍，突然一個小朋友跌進大水缸裏，將會淹死，司馬光情急智生，用一塊大石打破瓦缸，水全都流出來，那個小朋友因此沒有淹死，可見司馬光能夠急中生智！

Never spoil a ship for a haporth of tar

參看
REFERENCE
本書正文的 Lose a ship for a halfpenny worth of tar

One good turn deserves another
感恩圖報

好心有好報 / 禮尚往來 / 投桃報李 / 善有善報

此英文成語的意思是得到別人的恩惠後，應該找機會回報那人（所謂"得人恩果千年記"）。

✦ 參看
REFERENCE

（明）張居正《答薊鎮巡撫周樂軒書》："兩河官軍，感恩圖報，當有激於衷矣。"

孫中山《敬告同鄉書》："今二子之遁逃外國而倡保皇會也，其感恩圖報之未遑，豈尚有他哉？"

張天翼《萬仞約‧兒女們》："並不是廉大爺賞識了他的學問他才感恩圖報。"

《戰國策》"馮諼客孟嘗君"

👤 你知道嗎
DO YOU KNOW?

《伊索寓言》裏有一個"獅子與小鼠"的故事 (*Aesop's Fables*, "The Lion and the Mouse")：

有一天，森林之王獅子睡覺時，被一隻小鼠吵醒。獅子捉着小鼠時，小鼠哀求獅子不要吃牠，並說會報答獅子。獅子當天心情好，放了小鼠，但嘲笑小鼠如何能夠報答牠？！怎料幾天之後，獅子遭獵人設下的繩網困着，（翌日獵人便會來捉獅子），晚上，獅子呼叫着，這個時候小鼠出現了，並用牠尖銳的牙齒咬斷麻繩，獅子遂能逃脫。這個寓言證明弱小的小鼠有可能、亦真的有能力報答森林之王的獅子。

據說印度的寓言也有類似的感人故事：*Pancatantra* ("Winning of Friends")：一羣小鼠咬破了繩網，救走了一隻大象！

美國作家 Kate Neely Festetits (1836-1900) 曾用這句諺語作為她的書名：*One Good Turn Deserves Another.*

Kate Neely Festetits 的其他名句包括："Action speaks louder than words."

Paper over the cracks with something (White-washing)
粉飾太平

此英文成語的意思是隱藏或掩飾已出現的問題。

Professor Mary Wright (Yale University) 的歷史名著 *The Last Stand of Chinese Conservatism: the T'ung-Chi Restoration, 1862-1874.* (Stanford: Stanford University Press, 1957) 指清末的同治維新只不過是 **"white-washing"** 粉飾太平而已，所以同治維新失敗了！

(後來清朝在中日甲午戰爭 (1894-1895) 慘敗給日本。)

Persuasion is more effective than force
壓迫力越大，反抗力越強

此英文成語的意思是施加壓力往往招致反抗。

《伊索寓言》裏有一個 "北風與太陽" 的故事 (*Aesop's Fables*, "The North Wind and the Sun")，講述北風與太陽爭論誰最具威力，它們最後同意比賽 — 誰能先使一位行人脫掉衣服，誰就勝出。北風首先大力吹，不斷吹，但行人卻把衣服裹得更緊，終於北風放棄了。之後，太陽散發出它的溫暖，令行人感到溫暖甚至炎熱，於是脫掉衣服，即是太陽勝出了！

這個寓言教訓我們：溫和的說服方法比強大的暴力更有效！所謂壓迫力越大，反抗力越強！

Play fast and loose with someone
反覆無常

此英文成語可能來自古代的一種遊戲，遊戲由操作的人把皮帶折成多個圈，讓遊戲玩家以為可以用叉子把這條皮帶牢牢釘在桌子上，但當操作的人拉開皮帶時，遊戲玩家才知道他並沒有成功釘牢皮帶，因此就輸了遊戲。中文也有類似的成語，如反覆無常，意思是指一些不負責任的人玩弄他人。

> **參看**
> **REFERENCE**
> 《三國演義》："操曰：'袁譚小子，反覆無常，吾難準信。'"
>
> （清）林則徐《批英國領事義律派參遜赴洋示令全繳鴉片稟》："該領事須知本大臣推誠誠諭，迅速懍遵，不得反覆無常，自取咎戾。"
>
> 巴金《家》十："哪個曉得是真是假？你們做少爺、老爺的都是反覆無常，不高興的時候，甚麼事情都做得出來。"

Practice makes perfect
熟能生巧

Tempering for hundred times makes steel

此英文成語用來鼓勵學習者要多練習以掌握某種技巧。中文也有類似成語，如熟能生巧，來自歐陽修的《賣油翁》，故事通過善於射箭的陳康肅將軍和街市的賣油翁之交談，說明一個人不應因為自己有一技之長（例如善於射箭）而驕傲，看不起街市的賣油翁！賣油翁多年以來天天酌油，熟能生巧，酌油的技術肯定比善射的陳康肅好！

《鏡花緣》第三一回："第九公不必談了。俗語說的:'熟能生巧。'"

秦牧《藝海拾貝·蒙古馬的雕塑》:"這道理,'耳濡目染,熟能生巧'幾個字,就盡夠說出個中奧妙了。"

孔厥《新兒女英續傳》第四章:"不怕學不會,只怕不肯鑽。工夫到了,自然熟能生巧。"

例子
EXAMPLES

An old professor finds it difficult for him to learn and use the computer, but his students tell him that if he uses the computer everyday, he will be able to learn it – **"practice makes perfect!"**
(一位老教授覺得學習和使用電腦很困難,但他的學生告訴他,若他每天都用電腦,他就會學懂的了 —"熟能生巧"嘛!)

Prevention is better than cure
預防勝於治療

Though the sun shines, leave not your cloak at home / Forewarned is forearmed / 防患未然 / 杜漸防微 / 有備無患

此英文成語表示事情發生之前先作準備總比事後補救好。

參看
REFERENCE

《左傳·襄十一年》:"居安思危,思則有備,有備無患。"

《漢書·外戚傳》:"事不當固爭,防禍於未然。"

杜漸防微
東漢和帝時,竇太后臨朝聽政,兄長竇憲更獨掌大權,一位大臣名叫丁鴻,上奏和帝,力陳竇憲的罪狀,並勸諫和帝防範弊

病須從小處着手，才不致釀成大禍（"杜漸防微"）！

The Bible, *New Testament*, *Matthew* (7:15)："Beware of false prophets, who come to you in sheep's clothing, but actually they are ravening wolves."（《聖經・新約》，《馬太福音》(7:15)："要防備假先知 — 他們外面披着羊皮，其實是殘暴的豺狼。"），這裏的意思是假先知是會出現的，必須小心防範。

例子
EXAMPLES

Every winter, the Department of Health of the Hong Kong Government always reminds the citizens to take Influenza Vaccine – "**prevention is better than cure!**"（每年冬季，香港政府的衛生署都會提醒市民要注射流行性感冒疫苗 — 因為"預防勝於治療！"）

Pull out all the stops
全力以赴

竭盡所能 / 全心全意 / 盡我所能

據說此英文成語與管風琴的結構有關，管風琴有一個像塞子的部份，可以控制空氣流動，拉起這個部份便可以提高音量，發出音響。

1865 年，Matthew Arnold 在 *Essays in Criticism* 曾經使用這句成語：

"Knowing how unpopular a task one is undertaking when one tries to pull out a few more stops in that... somewhat narrow-toned organ, the modern Englishman."

中文也有類似的成語，如"全力以赴"，表示傾盡全力，做到
最好。

★ 參看
REFERENCE
(清)·趙翼《廿二史札記》："蓋當時薦舉徵辟；必采名譽；故
凡可以得名者；必全力赴之；好為苟難；遂成風俗。"
峻青《秋色賦·故鄉雜記》："在那艱苦的戰鬥的日子裏，解放
區的全體人民，心都緊緊地扭在一起，團結得像一個人似的，
全力以赴的對付敵人。"

Put the cart before the horse
本末倒置

Turn things upside down / The first and last turn around

此英文成語的意思是做事要分輕重及緩急先後。

★ 參看
REFERENCE
John Heywood's *A Dialogue Conteinyng the Nomber in Effect of All
the Prouerbes in the Englishe Tongue*. [*A Dialogue Containing the
Number in Effect of All the Proverbs in the English Tongue*] (1589):

"To tourne [turn] the cat in the pan, or **set the cart before the hors
[horse].**"

《戰國策·齊策》："書未發，威后問使者日：'問歲亦無恙耶？
民亦無恙耶？王亦無恙耶？'""故有問，'舍本而問末者耶？'"

▲ 你知道嗎
DO YOU KNOW?
戰國時，齊襄王派使臣訪趙國。趙威后接過齊襄王的書信，
還未拆開，便問使者："貴國的收成好嗎？百姓好嗎？國君好
嗎？"使臣很不高興地回答："威后為何先問候敝國的收成和百

姓，最後才是君王，豈非卑賤與尊貴倒置？"

趙威后正色道："你這樣想便錯了！沒有收成便沒有百姓，沒有百姓便沒有君王！所以我才這樣問，難道要本末倒置嗎？！"

Pyrrhic victory
慘勝

源於古羅馬歷史的 Punic Wars。

Pyrrhus 是出色的希臘將軍，精於戰術，在 280 B.C. 的 Punic Wars, Carthage（迦太基）軍隊請 Pyrrhus 幫忙，出動戰象擊敗羅馬軍，但損兵折將，結果可算是慘勝。

你知道嗎
DO YOU KNOW?

現在 Pyrrhus's victory 或 Pyrrhic victory，意思是付出極大代價的慘勝、得不償失的勝利、代價高的慘勝。

例子
EXAMPLES

The Allies fought back on June 6, 1944 in Normandy, causing immense casualties on both sides. The Allies won, but it was a **Pyrrhic victory**! (1944 年 6 月 6 日，盟軍反攻德軍，登陸諾曼第，雙方死傷慘重，盟軍可說是慘勝。)

Que Sera Sera (French)
(Whatever will be will be)

★ 參看
REFERENCE
本書正文的 Come what (come) may

Quos Deus vult perdere, prius dementat (Latin)
Whom God wishes to destroy, he first makes the man mad
神要毀滅人,必先令他瘋狂。

來自古希臘悲劇家 Euripedes (480-406 B.C.)

(one of the three great ancient Greek tragedians), Fragments.

Reading between the lines
字裏行間

此英文成語是指仔細閱讀文章的內容及隱含的意思。

例子
EXAMPLES

Aesop's Fables seem to be simple stories for children, however, if we carefully **read between the lines**, we may learn a lot of hidden wisdom from the fables. (《伊索寓言》似乎是小孩子的簡單故事,不過,若我們細心閱讀其字裏行間的意思,我們可能會學到很多隱藏的智慧。)

Rome was not founded in one day (Rome was not built in a day)
羅馬並非一日建成的

The best fruits are slowest in ripening / 大器晚成 / 老子:"大方無隅,大器晚成" / 十年樹木,百年樹人

意思是凡事不可操之過急,要有耐心才能成事。

你知道嗎
DO YOU KNOW?

根據古羅馬的經典 Virgil, *Aeneid:* 羅馬的創建者 Romulus 在 Tiber River 旁建造羅馬城,但開始時遭遇很多困難和挫折,不過,羅馬城終於成為橫跨歐、亞、非三大洲的羅馬帝國之首都。這句成語比喻大事業的建立並非一日而成。

西班牙中古時期名作家 Cervantes (1547-1616) 之名著《唐吉訶德》(*Don Quixote*) 亦曾引此名句。

When Tommy was not successful in an interview, he felt upset and was frustrated. His teacher tried to encourage him and told him that "**Rome was not founded in one day**." (當湯美面試失敗，他感到挫敗，他的老師鼓勵他："羅馬也非一日建成的！")

Run out of steam / gas
筋疲力盡

力竭筋疲 / 力盡筋疲 / 筋疲力竭

據說這句成語源於舊式蒸汽機的操作，這種蒸汽機會因火力減低而致速度變慢，最後會停下來。

1898 年，美國愛荷華州 (Iowa) 的一份報紙 *The Perry Daily Chief* 已曾經使用這句成語："...that made it impossible for me to get in one word to her hundred. I stood it for a little while in hope she would **run out of steam** or material, but she gathered force as she went."

參看
REFERENCE
《官場現形記》："趙家一門大小，日夜忙碌，早已弄得筋疲力盡，人仰馬翻。"
老舍《不成問題的問題》："說到這裏，他彷彿已筋疲力盡，快要暈倒的樣子。"

Saying is one thing and doing another

知易行難

That's easier said than done

能說不等於能做，（講就容易，做起來就難了），提醒人別隨便誇口。

例子
EXAMPLES

When the students boast that they can do almost everything, the teacher kindly reminds them "**saying is one thing and doing another**" or "that's easier said than done." （當學生誇耀他們幾乎甚麼都可以做的時候，老師提醒他們 "知易行難" 啊！）

Seek and you shall find

參看
REFERENCE

本書附錄一的 *Cerca Trova*

Seize the day

參看
REFERENCE

本書附錄一的 *Carpe Diem*

Si fueris Romae, Romano vivito more;
Si fueris alibi, vivito sicut ibi. (Latin)

參看
REFERENCE
本書正文的 Do in Rome as the Romans do

Silence is golden (Silence is gold)
沉默是金

據說曾經有一個小國到中國進貢了三個金人，但是使節出了一個難題："這三個一模一樣的金人哪個最有價值呢？"皇帝不懂，最後，一位老臣子想了一個方法 — 老臣拿出三根稻草分別從金人的耳中插入：第一根稻草從金人的另一邊耳朵出來了；第二個金人的稻草從嘴巴裏直接掉出來；而第三個金人，稻草進去之後掉入肚中，沒有任何聲音。老臣即說道："第三個金人最有價值！"這個故事教訓我們：要多聽取別人的意見，謹言慎行，不要隨便發表意見，只有多聞慎言，沉默是金，才是最好、最有價值的！如果不能保持沉默，那就會言多必失了。

六十年代由 The Tremeloes 主唱的一首流行曲，名字就是
"Silence Is Golden"

"Silence Is Golden"

Oh *don't it hurt deep inside
To see someone do something to her
Oh *don't it pain to see someone cry
How especially if that someone is her

Silence is golden

But my eyes still see

Silence is golden, golden

…

* 注：don't it 雖然不符合英語文法，但此為歌詞原文。

而香港的流行曲亦有"沉默是金"（作詞：許冠傑；作曲：張國榮）：

"沉默是金"

夜風凜凜獨回望舊事前塵 是以往的我充滿怒憤

誣告與指責積壓着滿肚氣不憤

對謠言反應甚為着緊

…

是錯永不對真永是真

任你怎說 安守我本分 始終相信沉默是金

**參看
REFERENCE**

Thomas Carlyle 把德文的 *Sartor Resartus* (1831) 翻譯成英文：

"Speech too is great, but not the greatest. As the Swiss Inscription says: *Sprecfien ist silbern, Schweigen ist golden* (Speech is silvern [silver], **Silence is golden**); or as I might rather express it: Speech is of Time, Silence is of Eternity."

Sour grapes
酸葡萄 / 吃不到的葡萄是酸的

此英文成語的意思是因得不到某物或達不到某目標而灰心，
推說那些事物或目標可能不值得自己努力追求。

你知道嗎
DO YOU KNOW?

《伊索寓言》有一個關於"酸葡萄"的故事 (*Aesop's Fables*, "The
Fox and the Bunch of Grapes") ：

一隻狐狸路過見到樹上的葡萄，狐狸嘗試跳上去摘葡萄，但並
不成功，經過多次嘗試失敗後，只好安慰自己說："那些葡萄是
酸的！"

這個寓言指出：有些人，因自己能力不足，只好推說那些目標
其實不是那麼好吧！

Still waters run deep
大智若愚

此英文成語可參看莎士比亞名劇《凱撒大帝》裏，凱撒大帝對
Cassius 的評價 (Julius Caesar's summing up of Cassius
in *Julius Caesar* (I.2.195-6)) ：

"Yon [That] Cassius hath [has] a lean and hungry look."

(意思是沉默的人是危險的 [Silent people are dangerous]).

參看
REFERENCE

The *Oxford Concise Dictionary of Proverbs*:

"*altissima quaeque flumina minimo sono labi*"

(the deepest rivers flow with least sound)

in *A History of Alexander the Great* by Quintus Rufus Curtius.

Peter is capable and knowledgeable, yet he looks simple and dresses simply. Most people do not recognize his potential and talents. Perhaps, "**still waters run deep!**"（彼得很能幹又博學，不過，他其貌不揚又衣著平凡。很多人都不知道他的潛能及才華。或者，這就是"大智若愚"吧！）

Survival of the fittest
物競天擇，適者生存（嚴復譯）

這句來自英國科學家達爾文 (Charles Darwin, 1809-1882) 的名著《物種起源》(*The Origin of Species,* Chapter 3)：

"It's not the strongest species that survive, nor the most intelligent, but the most responsive to change." （即是："能生存的物種不是最強的，也不是最有智慧的，而是最能適應（變化）的。"）

你知道嗎
DO YOU KNOW?
社會達爾文主義在十九、二十世紀深深影響着新帝國主義（包括優生學及希特拉）。

That's easier said than done

✳ 參看
REFERENCE
本書正文的 Saying is one thing and doing another.

That's Greek to me

✳ 參看
REFERENCE
本書附錄一的 It's Greek to me

The golden mean
中庸之道

來自古希臘哲學家 Aristotle（阿里士多德），他認為道德行為是兩極端 — 過多（過度）與過少（不足）— 之中庸。中庸之道就是道德。

你知道嗎
DO YOU KNOW?

希臘神話中，Daedelus 和 Icarus 父子用蠟製鳥毛的翼，飛離 King Minos 的小島，Daedelus 提醒兒子要飛於中間路線 (fly the middle course)（中庸之道），因為飛得太高，蠟會被太陽熔化；飛得太低，會被海水影響，但兒子 Icarus 太興奮了，越飛越高，終於翼的蠟被太陽熔化，Icarus 終於掉下海而死。

中國儒家 (Confucianism) 亦有中庸之道的哲學。Professor John King Fairbank 認為儒家在中國歷史中十分成功，主要就是其中庸之道 (moderation and balance) 的哲學，尤其是相比於無為的道家與進取的法家，儒家亦正是在中間。(參看 John King Fairbank and others, *East Asia: Tradition and Transformation*. Boston: Houghton Mifflin, 1978, p. 46).

The history of the world is but the biography of great men
(世界的歷史只是偉人的傳記)

這句來自 Thomas Carlye (1795-1881), *Heroes and Hero-Worship, I, "The Hero as Divinity"*：

Carlye 認為人類自古以來 (從神話時代到當代) 都喜歡英雄崇拜，所以，世界的歷史只是偉人的傳記。

其實，中國的司馬遷《史記》何嘗不是偉人的傳記呢？

(《史記》的本紀是帝王的傳記；世家是貴族的傳記；列傳 (例如：荊軻列傳) 是英雄的傳記)。

清末，曾國藩《聖哲畫像記》教兒子曾紀澤選一或多位聖哲，集中研習他們的文章、思想，跟隨這些聖賢便會成才。

(結果，曾紀澤亦算成才 ─ 他後來出任清廷駐俄羅斯的大使。)

The leopard does not change his spots

江山易改，本性難移

What is bred in the bone will never come out of the flesh / You cannot make a crab walk straight / Once a knave and always a knave / The fox changes his skin but not his habits / 萬變不離其宗 / 死性不改

此句以豹不會改變皮上的斑點比喻一個人本性難改。

參看 REFERENCE

The Bible, Old Testament, Jeremiah, (13:23)："Can the Ethiopian change his skin? **The leopard his spots**?"（《聖經·舊約》《耶利米書》(13:23)："雇士（古實）人豈能改變他的膚色，豹子豈能改變牠的斑點？"）

例子 EXAMPLES

Donald Trump was a businessman. Even after he became the President of the United States of America, his ways of doing things have not changed – "**the leopard does not change his spots**!"（特朗普是個商人，他做了美國總統之後，處事的作風仍然沒有改變 — 真是"江山易改，本性難移！"）

Pride comes / goes before a fall
骁兵必敗

此句的意思是切莫驕傲，不然就會招致失敗。

《伊索寓言》裏有一個 "龜兔賽跑" 的故事 (*Aesop's Fables*, "The Tortoise and the Hare")：

烏龜和兔子比賽，看誰能以最快速度跑到目的地，兔子跑到一半，回頭見到烏龜遠遠在後面爬着，便決定小睡片刻，但當兔子睡醒時，烏龜已到達目的地，並贏了比賽！

這個伊索寓言教訓我們不要驕傲，只有不斷努力才是成功之道，像烏龜雖動作緩慢，但堅定前行 (slowly but surely)，最終贏了兔子！(Hard work may prevail over natural talents, especially when the talent is too proud.)

後來，有些人又加了兩個頗有創意的續集：第二次比賽兔子不驕傲了，努力跑到終點，贏回一次。第三次比賽的路徑卻要經過一條河，兔子不懂得游水過河，烏龜卻可以，最後，烏龜讓兔子坐在牠的背上過河，大家互相幫助，互補不足，成為雙贏的好朋友！

There is no place like home
在家千日好 / 世上沒有比家更好的地方

這句來自 Frank Baum (1856-1919) 的著名兒童小說《綠野仙蹤》*Wizard of Oz* (1939)：

"There is no place like home" 是女主角 — 小女孩 Dorothy 經歷 Land of Oz 的驚險之後，準備回到 Kansas 家的時候，對朋友說的話。

現在我們日常生活中，也常用這句（中英文）來表達在家的好！

故事《綠野仙蹤》被拍成電影，十分受歡迎，其中主題曲 "Somewhere over the Rainbow" (by Judy Garland) 更成為經典兒歌：

"Somewhere over the Rainbow"

Somewhere over the rainbow, way up high
There's a land that I've heard of once in a lullaby.
Somewhere over the rainbow, skies are blue
And the dreams that you dare to dream,
Really do come true.

…

**例子
EXAMPLES**

After travelling around the world for a month, Peter and his family return home, and they all exclaim that **"there is no place like home!"** （環遊世界一個月後，彼得和家人終於回家了，大家都慨歎 "世上沒有比家更好的地方！"）

There's many a slip between the cup and the lip
天有不測之風雲

Although the sun shines, leave not your cloak at home. / Don't count your chickens before they hatch.

這句來自希臘神話 The Argonauts: 有一個先知警告 Ancaeus — 他出戰後，將不能嘗到他的葡萄園之果實。不過，他平安回來了，於是他想往找那個先知，但這個時候，一隻野豬出現在他的葡萄園，Ancaeus 趕去卻遭野豬殺死，所以，他正如先知的預言 / 警告 — 果然未能嚐到他的葡萄園之果實！

There is no such thing as a free lunch
這個世界沒有免費的午餐 / 沒有白吃的事

那有咁大隻蛤蟆隨街跳 ?!

此成語是指我們有時會貪心，希望可以免費得到一些東西，例如午餐。這句說話提醒我們：得到東西往往是要付出代價的。

你知道嗎
DO YOU KNOW?

諾貝爾經濟學得獎學者 Milton Friedman (1912-2006)，亦曾用這句作為他的一本書的書名 — *There is No Such Thing as a Free Lunch* (1975)。

Time flies
光陰似箭，日月如梭 / 時間過得真快

時光飛逝 / How time flies! / Time flies like an arrow

例子
EXAMPLES

At a reunion party for the alumni of a renowned university, most alumni, who graduated 30 years ago, exclaimed, "**How time flies!**" (在一間著名大學的舊生重聚晚會，很多畢業了三十年的舊生都慨歎："時光飛逝！" (時間過得真快))

Time is money
時間就是金錢

一寸光陰一寸金 (寸金難買寸光陰)

此成語來自富蘭克林 (Benjamin Franklin, 1706-1790), *Advice to A Young Trademan* (1748)：

"Remember that time is money." (記住時間就是金錢。)

> **參看**
> **REFERENCE**
>
> 古希臘哲學家泰奧弗拉斯托斯 Theophrastus (370-285 B.C.), *Lives and Opinions of Eminent Philosophers*《名哲言行錄》：
>
> "Time is the most valuable thing a man can spend." (一個人能花的最寶貴東西就是時間。)

Tip of the iceberg
冰山一角

十份之九的冰山是在海水下面，在海水上面的只是十份之一，所以，此成語冰山一角 (**Tip of the iceberg**) 的意思是表面上很少的，其實下面 (或內裏) 可以很大。

> **你知道嗎**
> **DO YOU KNOW?**
>
> 二十世紀初，當時世界上最大的郵輪鐵達尼號 (The Titanic) 便是撞到冰山而沉沒 (荷里活亦把這段歷史故事拍成電影)。
>
> 根據希臘神話，大地之母 Gaia 與 Uranus 生下的第二代就是十二個巨人 (Titans)，所以，Titanic 就是有巨人、巨大的意思。

To err is human (to forgive, humane)
犯錯誤乃人性，寬恕是神性

人誰無過 /（過）錯而能改，善莫大焉

此成語最早來自拉丁古訓：*"Humanum est errare"* (Latin)

後來十六世紀英國詩人亞歷山大·蒲柏 (Alexander Pope, 1688-1744)，*An Essay on Criticism* (1709)：

"To err is human, to forgive humane"

此句的意思是犯錯乃人之常情，而基督宗教而言，神會寬恕人的過錯，所以我們應該寬恕別人。後來傳誦一時，成為名人名句。

例子 EXAMPLES

A Catholic sinned and he went to a Catholic Father for confession. The Catholic Father kindly forgave him and said, "**To err is human (to forgive, humane)**." （一名天主教徒犯了罪，於是他向一個神父告解，那神父寬恕了他並仁慈地說："犯錯誤乃人性，寬恕是神性。"）

United we stand, divided we fall
團結就是力量

Union (unity) is strength / 齊心就事成 / 二人同心，其利斷金 / 眾志成城

此成語的意思是齊心才事成。

在美國甘迺迪總統的就職演講 (President John F. Kennedy's Inaugural Speech, January, 1961) 裏，他用了不同的方式表達團結的巨大力量：

"United, there is little we cannot do, ... Divided there is little we can do. ..." (請參看 William Safire, ed., *Lend Me Your Ears: Great Speeches in History*. New York: W.W. Norton, 2004, pp. 969-973.)

而哲學家 Francis Bacon (培根) 亦有類似之名句 "Strength united is the greater" (力量因團結而更強)。

中國民間也會唱誦團結的可貴，有一首兒歌名為 "一枝竹仔"，亦有這個意思：

一枝竹仔易折彎，幾枝一紮斷折難

心堅志毅勇敢團結方可有力量！

…

★ 參看
REFERENCE

《國語 · 周語下》：

"眾心成城，眾口鑠金。"

古希臘荷馬《伊利亞德》Homer, *Iliad:* "Union gives strength, even to weak men."

("即使弱者，亦因團結而得到力量。")

DO YOU KNOW?

《伊索寓言》裏有一個"父親和他的兒子們"的故事 (*Aesop's Fables*, "The Ploughman's Quarrelsome Sons")：

有一個父親，見到他的幾個兒子常常吵架。有一天，他叫他的兒子各自折斷一枝柴枝，他們都很易做到。之後，父親叫他們各自折斷一捆柴枝，這次，他們都不能做到。父親就向他們說："若他們不斷爭吵，便會逐一被折斷，不過，若他們團結起來，便不會被折斷了！"

另一個故事來自《魏書》，記載突谷渾的首領阿豺，他的兒子常常吵架。阿豺恐防因此而失國，就利用折箭的道理說明兄弟要像一捆箭一般同心協力，才不會被敵人"折斷"(打敗)。

據說成吉思汗 (Genghis Khan) 亦有類似的故事。

When in Rome, live as the Romans do; when in elsewhere, live as they live elsewhere

參看
REFERENCE
本書正文的 Do in Rome as the Romans do

When things are at the worst, they will mend
否極泰來

參看
REFERENCE
本書附錄一的 If winter comes, will spring be far behind?

Where there is a will, there is a way
有志者事竟成

此成語是指若一個人有決心，他會盡力克服困難以完成事情。

(If a person is really determined, he will try his best to overcome the obstacles and succeed.)

參看
REFERENCE
George Herbert's "Jacula Prudentusm" (1640):

"To him that will, ways are not wanting."

New Monthly Magazine (1822):

"Where there is a will, there is a way."

Yesterday's man
今非昔比

Yesterday's news 過時陳舊，不合潮流

此英文成語形容一個人的職業生涯從頂峰落入了低谷，甚至瀕臨結束邊緣，較常用於形容政客。

七十年代一首英文流行民歌 **"Streets of London"**，內容諷刺英帝國衰落，也有類似歌詞：

"Streets of London"

Have you seen the old man

In the closed-down market

Kicking up the paper

With his worn out shoes?

In his eyes you see no pride

Hand held loosely at his side

Yesterday's paper telling yesterday's news

...

Yes and No
不置可否

模棱兩可

此英文成語的意思是對某部份同意，但對另一部份則不同意，（既是但也不是），通常用於回答問題。

參看
REFERENCE

The Enigma Variations "Do you believe that if you continue seeing me you'll be damned?" "**Yes and no**."

例子
EXAMPLES

Scholars like to laugh at some diplomats, who always answer too tactfully without letting you know what they really think – for instance, if they say "yes", they may mean "perhaps", if they say "perhaps", they probably means "no". If someone answers "no", then that person is not a diplomat! (學者喜歡嘲笑一些外交家，他們常常有技巧地答得不置可否，令外人不知道他們真正的想法，例如：若他們答 "是" 的時候，他們可能只是表示 "或者"，若他們答 "或者" 時，他們其實是說 "不"！ 不過，那人若說 "不"，他就不是外交家了 (不夠圓滑)！)

When Donald Trump was asked whether he has good relationship with China, he answered, "**Yes and no** – on the one hand, I respect President Xi of China, but on the other hand, I believe that China has been gaining a lot of money from America." (當 Donald Trump 被問及他與中國是否關係良好時，他答道："**Yes and no** (既是但也不是)，一方面，我尊敬習主席，但另一方面，我又覺得中國長期賺取美國的金錢。")

If you ask some diplomats whether they support the Chief Executive. They may answer skilfully, "**Yes and no** – on the one hand, the Chief Executive is quite good in certain policies, yet, on the other hand, the Chief Executive has some flaws, too. (若你問一些外交家會否支持特首？外交家會答得很有技巧 (模棱兩可) — "**Yes and no**" — 一方面，特首的一些政策頗好，但另一面，特首亦有些瑕疵。)

Zip your lip

此英文成語的意思是保持緘默，不再出聲，不表意見。

to stop talking

to stay calm

to stay hush

to remain secret or silent

例子 EXAMPLES

Peter zipped his lip at the meeting yesterday, as it was pointless to say anything – as the meeting was dominated by the Chairman and his followers.（彼德在昨天的會議中保持緘默，不表意見，因為會議被主席及他的追隨者完全控制，講甚麼都沒有用。）

你知道嗎 DO YOU KNOW?

十九世紀時，此英文成語是 "button your lips"，因為當時是用鈕 (button) 來扣緊衫褲，到二十世紀，拉鍊 (zipper) 取代鈕，此英文成語亦變為 "zip your lip" 了。

Famous Quotes by Great Men
名人名句

A thing of beauty is a joy forever.
美的事物是永恆的喜悅。

來自英國詩人濟慈 (John Keats, 1795-1821) 的〈恩底彌翁〉 (Endymion) (內容源自古希臘神話)：

Endymion 是英俊的牧羊人，月亮女神 Selene (在詩中名叫 Cynthia) 愛上他，於是 Selene 求眾神之神宙斯 (Zeus) 令 Endymion 永遠俊美，宙斯卻令他永遠沉睡 — 因而 Endymion 與 Selene 永遠在一起，而他的俊美亦成為永恆的喜悅。

Achilles' heel

意思是致命傷 (fatal point)。

阿基利斯的腳踝，源自古希臘神話，荷馬史詩 Iliad《伊利亞特》(又稱《木馬屠城記》) 的英雄 Achilles，他母親是海洋女神 Thetis (忒提斯)，Achilles 出生後，Thetis 手執 Achilles 的腳踝，浸在冥府之 River Styx (怨恨河)，令他全身刀槍不入 —— 除了他的腳踝，因而 Achilles' heel 是他的 "致命傷"，即 fatal point。當 Achilles 殺死 Troy (特洛依) 王子 Hector (赫克托爾) 時，特洛依的士兵不斷向他射箭，本來都沒有用，但其中一枝箭卻射中他的腳踝，即他的 "致命傷"，而導致他死亡。

你知道嗎 DO YOU KNOW?

英國球星 Beckham 在球場上，遭人踢中腳跟，他倒地時大叫："Oh! My Achilles' heel!"

荷里活曾多次把 Achilles 的神話故事拍成電影，例如 2004 年的電影 Troy (〈特洛伊：木馬屠城〉)，由 Brad Pitt (畢彼特) 飾演 Achilles。

參看 REFERENCE

Samuel Taylor Coleridge, *The Friend; a literary, moral and political weekly paper.* (1810):

"Ireland, that vulnerable heel of the British Achilles!"

Ask not what your country can do for you, ask what you can do for your country!

不要問國家可以為你做甚麼，(應該)問你可以為國家做甚麼！

來自美國甘迺迪總統的就職演講 (President John F. Kennedy's Inaugural Speech, January 1961)。

你知道嗎
DO YOU KNOW?

古希臘的政治家 Pericles (ancient Athenian statesman) 曾說："I saw what the polis may do for her citizens, and what the citizens may do for their polis." (我看到城邦可以為它的公民做甚麼，又看到公民可以為他們的城邦做甚麼。)

據說替 President John F. Kennedy 寫稿的 Ted Sorensen 是受 Pericles 的名句啟發而寫出 President Kennedy 的就職演講名句。(請參看 William Safire, ed., *Lend Me Your Ears: Great Speeches in History*. New York: W.W. Norton, 2004, pp. 969-973.)

At sixes and sevens

參看
REFERENCE
本書前面正文的 At sixes and sevens

Beware the Ides of March！

小心提防三月十五日！

來自莎士比亞名劇《凱撒大帝》(William Shakespeare, 1564-1616, Julius Caesar)：

古羅馬歷史，44 B.C. 3 月 15 日，凱撒大帝 (Julius Caesar, 100 – 44 B.C.) 被其他元老刺殺，其實，事前他自己亦有預感。在莎士比亞名劇中，更有預言者向他警告：“Caesar！Beware the Ides of March!" (小心 / 提防三月十五日！)。

後來這句說話亦成為提示他人之警告，表示可能有不吉利的壞事發生。

Blood, toil, tears, and sweat
熱血、勞累、眼淚及汗水。

來自英國首相邱吉爾 (Winston Churchill) 對抗希特拉 (Hitler) 之飛彈轟炸的名句，每天在英國廣播公司 (BBC) 向英國國民演講，曾承認自己只有熱血、勞累、眼淚及汗水 ("I have nothing to offer but blood, toil, tears and sweat.")，但他亦強調英國仍會作戰到底，絕不放棄！

1962 年，荷里活有一套電影〈碧血長天〉 ("The Longest Day")，主題曲 "The Longest Day" (composed, written and sung by Paul Anka)，亦有這句歌詞：

"The Longest Day"

…

The longest day the longest day
This will be the longest day
Filled with hopes and filled with fears
Filled with **blood and sweat and tears**

…

〈碧血長天〉("The Longest Day") 是 1962 年的荷里活電影，講述第二次世界大戰 1944 年 6 月 6 日盟軍反攻德國在諾曼第 (Normandy) 登陸的戰役 — 戰況慘烈，雙方死傷慘重！之後亦有多套荷里活電影拍攝這場著名的戰役，例如：〈紅色警戒〉("The Thin Red Line")，〈雷霆救兵〉("Saving Private Ryan") 等。

Carpe Diem (Latin)

> ✴ 參看
> **REFERENCE**
> 本書前面正文的 Carpe Diem (Latin)

Cerca Trova. (Latin)
Seek and you shall find.

向主尋求，就會得到。

來自《聖經・新約》，《馬太福音》(7:7)：
意思是："我們只要向主尋求，就會得到我們所欲所求。"

> ⚠ 你知道嗎
> **DO YOU KNOW?**
> 現在這句甚至擴展至非宗教的領域。

Cogito Ergo Sum (Latin)

> ✴ 參看
> **REFERENCE**
> 本書前面正文的 *Cogito Ergo Sum* (Latin)

Come what (come) may

✱ 參看
REFERENCE
本書前面正文的 Come what (come) may

Crossing the river by feeling the stones
摸着石頭過河

Wade the river by groping for stones / Advance step by step

這是改革開放初期鄧小平之名句："表示中國仍在向前探索，但會努力向前。"

Deeply regret (diplomatic term)

✱ 參看
REFERENCE
本書前面正文的 Deeply regret (diplomatic term)

Energy and persistence conquer all things.
能量和堅持 (毅力) 征服一切。

來自富蘭克林 (Benjamin Franklin, 1706-1790) 的名句。

富蘭克林認為："要達至我們的目標，我們必須要有能量和堅持 (毅力)。"。 "To achieve our goal (s), we should have energy and persistence."

Et tu, Brute?
And you, Brutus?

布魯圖,還有您呢?

來自莎士比亞名劇〈凱撒大帝〉(William Shakespeare, 1564-1616, Julius Caesar):

古羅馬歷史:44 B.C. 的 3 月 15 日,凱撒大帝 (Julius Caesar, 100 – 44 B.C.) 被其他元老刺殺。其實,事前凱撒自己亦有預感。在莎士比亞名劇中,那天凱撒本來不想去元老院,但 Brutus 卻親自一早到凱撒的家,不斷遊說並陪同凱撒前往元老院。這句 *"Et tu, Brute?"* 是凱撒死前最後的話 — 當眾元老各插凱撒一刀時,布魯圖卻心虛地躲在後面,於是凱撒走往布魯圖面前,說這句 *"Et tu, Brute?"* 布魯圖只好也插凱撒一刀,讓凱撒斷氣死去。

你知道嗎
DO YOU KNOW?
現在這名句亦有指斥 "背叛者" 的意思。

Eureka!
I have found it!

古希臘文,後來亦成拉丁文,意思是:"我發現了!"

古希臘學者阿基米德 (Archimedes, 287 – 212 B.C.) 洗澡時,在浴缸浸入身體時溢出水,因而悟出浮力理論及其原理,據說他當時驚歎道,"Eureka!"

("I have found it" 即是 "我發現了!")

Archimedes（阿基米德）是古希臘的物理、數學大師，古希臘文的意思是 "contemplating、pondering（深思、思考）"。

阿基米德出生於西西里島東南部的 Syracuse（敍拉古），較早時 Plato（柏拉圖）也曾前往該地教學。在阿基米德的時代，西西里島是地理戰略及政治要地，該地有活躍的火山，亦是三次 Punic Wars（布匿戰爭）的戰略島嶼。

他的阿基米德原理（Archimedes' Principle），對浮力作出了解說。船泊負荷多少，決定吃水多深，背後的規律就是阿基米德原理。

今天用 Archimedes' lever（阿基米德的槓桿）比喻強而有力的手段或方法。⇄

Experience is not what happens to you; it's what you do with what happens to you.

經驗不是甚麼發生在你身上，而是你如何面對這些事件。

來自赫胥黎 (Aldous Huxley, 1894-1963, author of *Brave New World*.) (《美麗的新世界》之作者)

赫胥黎其他相類似的名句 (similar ideas and sentences by Aldous Huxley)：

"Experience teaches only the teachable," Tragedy and the Whole Truth.

"That men do not learn very much from the lessons of history is the most important of all the lessons that history has to teach," "A Case of Voluntary Ignorance," Collected Essays (1959).

Fiat lux. (Latin)
Let there be light.
Motto of the University of California

(加州大學校訓)

來自《聖經 · 舊約》,《創世記》*The Bible, Old Testament,* (Genesis, 1:3):

"And God said, let there be light: and there was light"。

你知道嗎
DO YOU KNOW?
很多英美大學因為有基督教的背景,所以校訓 (Motto) 都與基督教的《聖經》有關,尤其是 "光" (lux) (light)。

Give a man a fish, feed him for a day.
Teach a man to fish, feed him for a lifetime.

參看
REFERENCE
本書前面正文的 Give a man a fish, feed him for a day. Teach a man to fish, feed him for a lifetime.

God, grant me the serenity to accept the things I cannot change,
Courage to change the things I can,
And wisdom to know the difference.

(神啊,請賜我平靜,讓我接受我無法改變的事情,

請賜我勇氣,讓我改變我能改變的事情,

請賜我智慧,讓我能區別以上兩者的不同。)

來自美國神學家尼布爾 (Reinhold Niebuhr, 1892-1971, an American theologian) 的 "寧靜禱文" ("The Serenity Prayer")。

He, who knows only his own side of the case, knows little of that.

只曉得自己觀點的人，其實所知無多。

來自密爾 (John Stuart Mill, 1806-1873), On Liberty.
《論自由》(1859)。

你知道嗎
DO YOU KNOW?
嚴復把 On Liberty 翻譯為《群己權界論》。

I have a dream.

我有一個夢。

來自美國民權領袖馬丁路德金牧師於 1964 年的著名演說 (Martin Luther King, Jr. 'Speech for the Civil Rights Movement at the Lincoln Memorial in 1964'):

"… I have a dream that my four little children will one day live in a nation where they will not be judged by the color of their skin but by the content of their character. ..."

("…我有一個夢：我的四個子女終有一天，會生活在一個國家 — 不會只看他們的膚色，而是以他們的性格內涵來評價他們。…")

西方的"夢（想）"亦可參考經典名曲 **"The Impossible Dream"**

(百老匯著名歌劇 Man of La Mancha 是有關西班牙中古武士唐吉訶德的追求夢想 — Don Quixote's the Quest):

"The Impossible Dream"

To dream **the impossible dream**

To fight the unbeatable foe

To bear with unbearable sorrow

To run where the brave dare not go

…

To reach the unreachable star

Cf. The American dream

I shall return.

我會回來

美國麥克阿瑟將軍 (General Douglas MacArthur, 1880-1964) 於第二次世界大戰之太平洋戰爭中，被日軍圍困，這句是他在 1942 年 3 月 11 日撤離菲律賓時之豪情壯語，表示一定會回來，並暗示會擊敗日軍。

If history repeats itself, first as a tragedy, second as a farce.

若歷史不斷重演，第一次是悲劇，再次就是鬧劇。

來自經濟學家馬克思 (Karl Marx, 1818-1883) 的《資本論》Das Kapital (1867)：

馬克思的《資本論》分析及批判資本主義 (capitalism)。他認為歷史常常重複發生，尤其是錯誤，因為人沒有從錯誤中學習！若第一次歷史重演，可以說是悲劇，但若不斷重複發生，屢錯不改，那就是鬧劇了！

If winter comes, will spring be far behind?

冬天來了，春天還會遠嗎？

來自浪漫主義詩人雪萊 (Percy Bysshe Shelley, 1792-1822) 的 *Ode to the West Wind* (1819)〈西風頌〉，他用西風來歌頌革命力量。這句說話表示他對未來的樂觀：冬天喻意困境，春天則是生機，即是當我們在困境時，生機也快來臨！

> **你知道嗎**
> **DO YOU KNOW?**
> 中國《易經》的"否極泰來"亦有這個意思。
> When things are at the worst, they will mend.

It's Greek to me.
"Graecum est; non legitu." (Latin)

我不懂。

That's Greek to me. / It's (all) Greek to me. / (意思是 something is not understandable) / It is Greek (therefore) it cannot be read.

來自莎士比亞白的名劇〈凱撒大帝〉(William Shakespeare, *The Tragedy of Julius Caesar* (1599))。其實，凱撒大帝 (Julius Caesar, 100–44 B.C.) 精通拉丁文之外，亦懂希臘文，不過，當他與人爭論而不願再談時，他會用這句說話 "it was Greek to me" (後來成為成語) — 推說自己不懂而終止討論！

CASSIUS: Did Cicero say any thing?

CASCA: Ay, he spoke Greek.

CASSIUS: To what effect?

CASCA: Nay, an I tell you that, I'll ne'er look you i' the face again: but those that understood him smiled at one another and shook their heads; but, for mine own part, **it was Greek to me**.

From William Shakespeare, *Julius Caesar.*

你知道嗎
DO YOU KNOW?
2011 年，香港商務印書館出版了一本《It's Not Greek to Me 必學英文 100 經典名句》，書名來自這名句。

Keep your face to the sunshine and you cannot see the shadow.

朝着陽光，你便看不見陰影。

來自聾啞瞎女作家海倫‧凱勒 (Helen Keller, 1880-1968), *The Story of My Life (1903)*。

聾啞瞎女作家海倫‧凱勒努力克服困難，(我們應該很容易想像到她所面對的困難)，不過，她卻鼓勵大家要樂觀 — 當我們面向陽光，就不會看到陰暗的事物，所以，我們要保持正面、堅強和樂觀。

Knowledge is power.
Scientia potential est. (Latin)

知識就是力量。

來自英國哲學家培根 (Francis Bacon, 1561-1626), *Meditationes Sacrae.* (1597)。

你知道嗎
DO YOU KNOW?
古希臘哲學家阿里士多德 (Aristotle) 亦曾說："The one exclusive sign of thorough knowledge is the power of teaching."

Let us never negotiate out of fear. But let us never fear to negotiate.

我們絕對不要因恐懼而去談判，但我們也絕對不要懼怕去談判。

來自美國甘迺迪總統的就職演講 (President John F. Kennedy's Inaugural Speech, January, 1961)。

當時一些甘迺迪之政敵（共和黨的鷹派）批評甘迺迪懦弱，因恐懼而去談判，所以，甘迺迪首先強調自己絕對不會因恐懼而去談判，不過，甘迺迪亦反擊，指出我們也絕對不應該懼怕去談判！

> **參看**
> **REFERENCE**
> William Safire, ed., *Lend Me Your Ears: Great Speeches in History*. New York: W.W. Norton, 2004, pp. 969-973.)

Nisi Dominus frustra. (Latin)
Without the Lord, everything is in vain.

沒有主，一切也是徒然。

來自《聖經‧舊約》，《詩篇》，*The Bible, Old Testament, Psalm* (127:1)

> **你知道嗎**
> **DO YOU KNOW?**
> 香港城門水塘亦有這句拉丁文。

One good turn deserves another.

善有善報。

> **參看**
> **REFERENCE**
> 本書前面正文的 One good turn deserves another.

Parting is such sweet sorrow (That I shall say goodnight till it be morrow).

離別是多麼甜蜜而傷感。

來自莎士比亞的名劇《羅密歐與茱麗葉》(William Shakespeare, *Romeo and Juliet*, II: ii, 184)。

荷里活電影 Romeo and Juliet，主題曲 "What is a youth" (theme song from *Romeo and Juliet*)：

What is a youth

Impetuous fire

…

例子
EXAMPLES

A few years ago, at a farewell party, Dr. Fred Cheung started his speech by quoting this famous Shakespeare's sentence from *Romeo and Juliet*, **"Parting is such sweet sorrow"** to bid farewell to the retiring staff. (數年前，在一個惜別會裏，張學明博士以莎士比亞名劇 *Romeo and Juliet* 的名句：「離別是多麼甜蜜而傷感」作為開場白，向退休的同事道別。)

Patience is bitter, but its fruit is sweet.

忍耐是艱苦的，不過它的果實是甜蜜的。

來自法國哲學家盧梭 (Jean Jacques Rousseau, 1712-1778, French philosopher, author of *The Social Contract.*) (《社會契約論》之作者)。

例子
EXAMPLES

Dr. Fred Cheung has been patiently promoting the study of history, culture and languages. The process was bitter. But for the past few years, he has published books such as《字源學英文》(*Learning English through Etymology*) and now《成語學英文》(*Learning English through Idioms*), we may say that **his fruits are sweet**. (張學明博士不斷耐性地提倡、推廣歷史、文化和語文的研讀，其過程是艱辛的，不過，過去幾年他出版了《字源學英文》，現又出版《成語學英文》，我們可以說：他的果實是甜蜜的。)

Power tends to corrupt, and absolute power corrupts absolutely.

權力導致腐化，絕對的權力肯定導致絕對的腐化。

來自英國歷史學家阿克頓 (Lord Acton (John Dalberg-Acton), 1834-1902, Historical Essays and Studies, Appendix)：

1887 年阿克頓給 (傳教士) 克萊頓 (Mandell Creighton, 1843-1901) 的一封信，提及這句。Lord Acton 認為權力導致人腐化，而擁有絕對權力的人，因為沒有人或其他制度制衡他，所以肯定會變得絕對的腐化！

Progress is the activity of today and the assurance of tomorrow.

進步是今天的行為活動及明天的保證。

來自美國思想家愛默生 (Ralph Waldo Emerson, 1803-1882, an American thinker)。

**例子
EXAMPLES**

Some students were frustrated because they did poorly in the midterm test. The teacher encouraged them to work harder now and they will surely have progress in the coming final examination, and the teacher quoted Emerson's famous saying, **"Progress is the activity of today and the assurance of tomorrow."** (一些學生感到挫敗因為他們在期中測驗考得很差。老師鼓勵他們現今要努力學習，他們肯定會在期終考試有進步，老師並引述愛默生的名句：" 進步是今天的行為活動及明天的保證。")

Quod nunc es fueram, famosus in orbe, viator, et quod nunc ego sum, tuque futurus eris. (Latin) You are now, traveller, what I once was, and what I am now you will one day become.

今夕吾軀歸故土，他朝君體也相同。

這名句是由羅馬帝王查理大帝 (Charlemagne) 的老師所寫的拉丁文詩句翻譯過來的，意思是人無法逃離死亡的現實，提醒我們要珍惜生命，放下對短暫生命的執着。

你知道嗎 DO YOU KNOW?

參看香港跑馬地聖彌額爾天主教墳場 (St. Michael Catholic Cemetery, Happy Valley, Hong Kong) 入口的對聯。

Quos Deus vult perdere, prius dementat. (Whom God wishes to destroy, he first makes the man mad.)

參看 REFERENCE

參看本書前面正文的 Quos Deus vult perdere, prius dementat.

Shangri-La
香格里拉，"世外桃源"

Shangri-La（香格里拉，又稱世外桃源），是源於 1933 年經典文學名著：James Hilton 的小說 *Lost Horizon*，後來亦拍成電影，片名是《消失的地平線》。故事講述一架飛機在尼泊爾（Nepal）山區墜毀，與外界隔絕三十多年，但乘客卻都保持青春不老。後來終於有人找回他們，但當他們返回歐洲後，卻發現自己不能保持青春，變老了三十多年，這讓他們十分懷念這個地方，遂稱這個地方為 Shangri-La，意思是"世外桃源"。

現在 Shangri-La 是指世外桃源、人間仙境。香港亦有兩間酒店名為 Shangri-La。

Singapore 亦有 Shangri-La 酒店，2018 年 6 月 12 日 美、朝 (Trump, U.S.A. / Kim, North Korea) 高峰會議，是 Trump 入住的酒店。

Si fueris Romae, Romano vivito more; Si fueris alibi, vivito sicut ibi. (Latin)

參看
REFERENCE
本書前面正文的 Do in Rome as the Romans do.

Some men see things as they are and say why, I dream things that never were and say why not?

一些人看見事情發生，只會歎息道：為甚麼 (點解) 呢？

(但) 我夢想到一些從未發生過的 (方法)，(而去嘗試 / 創新)，當其他人質疑我的時候，我會回答道：為甚麼不能呢？！

Made famous by Senator Robert Kennedy (羅拔 · 甘迺迪參議員)，1925-1968，originally written by Irish playwright George Bernard Shaw (愛爾蘭大文豪蕭伯納)，"Back to Methuselah" (1921), Part 1, Act 1)) :

"I hear you say 'why?' Always 'Why?' You see things; and you say 'Why?' But I dream things that never were; and I say 'Why not?' "

例子 EXAMPLES

Some men always complain that the study of history is boring. Dr. Fred Cheung has dreamed of teaching history through songs, movies and speeches. At first, some people might doubt if it works, but Fred answers confidently, "why not?!" (一些人經常投訴研讀歷史很沉悶，張學明博士夢想到通過歌曲、電影和演說來研讀歷史。最初，有人質疑其效果，但張學明充滿自信地回答：為甚麼不能呢？！)

Stay hungry, stay foolish.

永不自滿，執着若愚。

求知若飢，虛心若愚。

永不放棄，擇善固執

來自蘋果公司前總裁喬布斯 (Steve Jobs, 1955–2011) 在 2005 年發表的演說。喬布斯以這名句來提醒我們不要容易滿足、不要自滿 — 我們要時常鞭策自己，不斷努力進取、勇於嘗試創新。(其實這名句最初 (於 1970 年代) 見於 Stewart Brand, *The Whole Earth Catalog*, (in mid-1970s)) 。

喬布斯的演說：... When I was young, there was an amazing publication called *The Whole Earth Catalog,* which was one of the bibles of my generation. It was created by a fellow named Stewart Brand ..., and he brought it to life with his poetic touch. ... Stewart and his team put out several issues of *The Whole Earth Catalog*, and then ... they put out a final issue. ... On the back cover of their final issue was a photograph of an early morning country road, ... Beneath it, were the words: "Stay Hungry. Stay Foolish." It was their farewell message as they signed off. Stay Hungry. Stay Foolish. And I have always wished that for myself. And now, as you graduate to begin anew, I wish that for you. **"Stay Hungry. Stay Foolish."**

That's one small step for a man, a giant leap for mankind.

我的一小步，是人類的一大步。

這是首位腳踏月球 (於 1969 年) 的美國太空人岩士唐 (Neil Armstrong) 之名句。

你知道嗎 DO YOU KNOW?

Youtube 有這個人類歷史性的片段。荷里活亦拍攝了多套有關美國登陸月球的電影。

The history of the world is but the biography of great men.

參看 REFERENCE

本書前面正文的 The history of the world is but the biography of great men.

The only way to have a friend is be one.

交朋友的唯一方法就是成為一個真心朋友。

來自美國散文家愛默生 (Ralph Waldo Emerson, (1803-1882), Essays: First Series, 1841.) 。

意思是如果你想找朋友，首先要自己真心對人，自己先成為一個真心的朋友！

There are three kinds of lies: lies, damned lies and statistics.

謊言有三種：謊言、糟透的謊言及統計數字。

來自英國首相迪斯雷利 (Benjamin Disraeli, 1804-1881) 所說的名句，記載於美國作家馬克‧吐溫 (Mark Twain, 1835-1910) 的書《我的自傳》*Chapters from My Autobiography in North American Review* (1906).

Disraeli 及 Mark Twain 都認為謊言及統計數字都常誤導人，有些是數字遊戲，其實都是有利自己的謊言。

There is no perfection. There are always rooms for improvement, and we should try our best to work harder and to be better.

沒有最好，只有更好。

2015 年 10 月 21 日，英國首相卡梅倫 (Cameron) 與中國國家主席習近平舉行聯合記者會，其間談及人權問題，習主席說："保護人權，沒有最好，只有更好。"

參看 REFERENCE

馬銀春 "沒有最好，只有更好"，意思是傑出的人不會把成就視為一個固定的完美終點，他們只會不斷改進，做到更好。

參看 REFERENCE

Stay hungry, stay foolish.

There is no place like home.

★ 參看
REFERENCE

本書前面正文的 There is no place like home.

There's no such thing as a free lunch.

★ 參看
REFERENCE

本書前面正文的 There's no such thing as a free lunch.

Time is money.

★ 參看
REFERENCE

本書前面正文的 Time is money.

To be or not to be, that is the question.

活着抑或是去死，才是問題。

（活着還是死去，這才是問題。）

（不知如何抉擇，做還是不做？！）

來自莎士比亞名劇《哈姆雷特》又名《王子復仇記》(William Shakespeare, 1564-1616, *Hamlet*)

這個悲劇的主角，丹麥王子哈姆雷特，得悉父王被母后和叔叔謀殺，不知如何面對 — 做還是不做的抉擇？！

To err is human (to forgive, humane).

參看
REFERENCE
本書前面正文的 To err is human (to forgive, humane).

Veni, Vidi, Vici. (Latin)
"I came, I saw, I conquered."
我來到，我見到，我征服。
Julius Caesar 凱撒大帝 (100 – 44 B.C.) 之名句

古羅馬凱撒大帝文武全才，拉丁文功力深厚（當年筆者在加州大學修讀拉丁文，Julius Caesar 的文章是必讀的！其 *Conquest of Gaul*《高盧戰紀》更是筆者的至愛！），又 Julius Caesar 南征北伐，除了征服高盧（現在的法國），亦征服了不列顛島 (Britain 現在的英國)。在英倫海峽彼岸對着不列顛島曾有此豪語："*Veni, Vidi, Vici*" (I came, I saw, I conquered)（我來到，我見到，我征服），意思是征服不列顛島（對他而言）易如反掌，手到拿來！此句被譽為有帝王氣派 ─ Julius Caesar 未王而王。更難得的是這三個動詞本來的 infinitive (*venire* to come, *videre* to see, *vincere* to conquer) 及現在式 (present tense) (*venio* I come, *video* I see, *vincere* I conquer) 都是沒有壓韻的，但過去式 (past tense) 則成為 *Veni, Vidi, Vici* 壓韻有聲，可見 Julius Caesar 之拉丁文的功力及文采！

videre (Latin) = to see

video (Latin) = I see

vidi (Latin) = I saw

vu (Latin) = I have seen

déjà vu (French) = already seen

你知道嗎
DO YOU KNOW?

毛澤東於 1930 年代寫的〈沁園春〉："江山如此嬌，引無數英雄競折腰。秦皇漢武，略輸文采，唐宗宋祖，稍遜風騷，一代天嬌，成吉思汗，只會彎弓射大雕。俱往矣！想風流人物，還看今朝！"亦被認為有帝王氣派。

You may deceive all the people part of the time, and part of the people all of the time, but not all of the people all of the time.

你可以在部份時間欺騙所有人，或全然欺騙一部份人，但你不能全然 (永遠 / 不斷) 欺騙所有人。

來自美國林肯總統 (Abraham Lincoln, 1809-1865) 的演講。

林肯總統認為謊言無法永遠欺騙所有人，謊言總會被揭穿，誠實做人處事才是正途。

Learning English through Greek and Latin
希臘文、拉丁文學英文

Amen **(Hebrew or Aramaic, then, Latin, now English)**
意思是確定、真實、肯定
(confirm, truth, truly, verily, certainly)
(例如：**Jesus, "Amen, amen, I say unto you, ..."**)

現在基督徒亦常說 Amen 表示確信、完全同意的意思。

A priori **(Latin)**
Relating an argument that suggests the probable effects of a cause
由因及果的

From the previous

拉丁文：a 意思是 from,
priori 意思是 what is before,
所以即是 from what is before

Ad hoc **(Latin)**

for a particular purpose (committee)

意思是 特設的，特定目的 (委員會)

(Limited in time; to this point)

Ad infinitum **(Latin)**

To infinity

永無止境

不斷發生 / 不知何時結束或終止 / Endlessly

Carpe Diem **(Latin)**

Seize the day

> ☀ 參看
> **REFERENCE**
> 本書前面正文的 *Carpe Diem* (Latin)

Cerca Trova **(Latin)**

Seek and you shall find

向主尋求，就會得到

> ☀ 參看
> **REFERENCE**
> 本書附錄一的 *Cerca Trova* (Latin)

Citius, altius, fortius **(Latin)**

Swifter, higher, stronger

更快、更高、更強

(The Olympic Motto)

Cogito Ergo Sum (Latin)

★ 參看
REFERENCE
本書前面正文的 *Cogito Ergo Sum* (Latin)

Deo gratias
Thanks be to God
感謝天主

Dominus vobis cum, et cum spiritus tuo
May the Lord be with you, and with your spirit, too.
願主與你同在，也與你的心靈同在。

Equus
Horse
馬

你知道嗎
DO YOU KNOW?
英文有很多字 Equ- 都與馬有關，例如：equestrian 馬的；騎術的；騎馬者；equestrianism 馬術；equestrienne 女騎師。

Fiat lux (Latin)
Let there be light

★ 參看
REFERENCE
本書附錄一的 *Fiat lux* (Latin)

Homo proponit, sed Deus disponit (Latin)

参看
REFERENCE

本書前面正文的 Man proposes and God disposes

Imperium in imperio
Empire within the empire
帝國內的帝國 (核心內另有核心)

参看
REFERENCE

Arthur Wright, *Buddhism in Chinese History*. (Stanford: Stanford University Press, 1959), p. 67:

書中指出唐朝的帝王控制着佛教，不容許佛教在唐帝國內自成一個帝國 (成為另一權力核心)；又請參看 Frederick Hok Ming Cheung (張學明), From Military Aristocracy to Royal Bureaucracy: Patterns of Consolidation in Two Medieval Empires. (PhD dissertation, University of California, Santa Barbara, 1983), p. 104.

Nisi Dominus frustra (Latin)

参看
REFERENCE

本書附錄一的 *Nisi Dominus frustra* (Latin)

Oremus pro invicem
Let us pray for each other
讓我們互相為大家祈禱

Persona non grata (**Latin**)

An unwelcome person

不受歡迎的人

例子
EXAMPLES

Donald Trump has been a persona non grata, so he was not invited to many activities by the American people. (很多美國人都不喜歡 Donald Trump，視他為"不受歡迎的人"，所以，很多活動都不邀請他參加。)

Quod nunc es fueram, famosus in orbe, viator, et quod nunc ego sum, tuque futurus eris (**Latin**)

You are now, traveller, what I once was, and what I am now you will one day become

今夕吾軀歸故土，他朝君體也相同

參看
REFERENCE

本書附錄一的 *Quod nunc es fueram, famosus in orbe, viator, et quod nunc ego sum, tuque futurus eris* (Latin)

Quos Deus vult perdere, prius dementat

Whom God wishes to destroy, he first makes the man mad

參看
REFERENCE

本書前面正文的 *Quos Deus vult perdere, prius dementat*

Si fueris Romae, Romano vivito more; Si fueris alibi, vivito sicut ibi. (Latin)

(When in Rome, live as the Romans do; when in elsewhere, live as they live elsewhere.)

※ 參看
REFERENCE

本書前面正文的 *Si fueris Romae, Romano vivito more; Si fueris alibi , vivito sicut ibi.* (Latin)

Veni, Vidi, Vici (Latin)
(I came, I saw, I conquered)

※ 參看
REFERENCE

本書附錄一的 *Veni, Vidi, Vici* (Latin)

Learning Medical Terms through Etymology
字源學醫學名詞

Achilles: Achilles' heel, Achilles' tendon

Achilles（阿喀琉斯，或譯阿基利斯），是古希臘荷馬史詩 Iliad（《伊利亞特》，又稱《木馬屠城記》）中之英雄。他母親是海洋女神 Thetis（忒提斯），Achilles 出生後，Thetis 手執 Achilles 的腳踝，浸在冥府之 River Styx（怨恨河），令他全身刀槍不入 —— 但他的腳踝除外。當 Achilles 殺死 Troy（特洛依）王子 Hector（赫克托爾）時，特洛依的士兵不斷向他射箭，本來都沒有用，因他是刀槍不入的，但其中一枝箭卻射中他的腳踝，即他的"致命傷"，而導致他死亡。

英文成語 Achilles' heel（阿基利斯的腳踝）源自 Achilles，意思是"致命傷"，即 fatal point，因為 Achilles 除了腳踝之外，全身刀槍不入。此外，醫學名詞 Achilles' tendon（腳跟腱）也源自這個字。

Achillea-yarrow 西洋蓍草，用於止血
(A kind of herbal medicine in Iliad)

荷馬史詩 Iliad (《伊利亞特》或《木馬屠城記》) 中的英雄 Achilles (阿喀琉斯)，使用 Achillea-yarrow (西洋蓍草) 止傷兵的血，現代的醫學亦證明此種蓍草有止血功效！古希臘人亦喜歡把這些蓍草放在枕下，他們相信可令人有甜蜜的美夢。⇄

Anaesthesia **(Latin) 麻醉**
意思是失去感覺 (loss of feeling)

希臘文 anaisthesia (意思是 lack of sensation)，
an- 意思是 "without" + aisthesis 意思是 "feeling"，
現在是手術時的麻醉。

Anatomy 解剖
(Study of the structure and function of the human body by dissection)

希臘文 anatomia，anatome 意思是 dissection，
即是剖開 cutting up。

Aphrodite / Venus

Aphrodite 阿佛洛狄忒，古希臘神話中之愛神，亦是得到 "金蘋果" 的最美麗女神，是羅馬神話的 Venus 維納斯，文藝復興時期的偉大藝術家 Leonado da Vinci 達文西也認為維納斯的身材比例是女性中最完美的。

雖然 Aphrodite 嫁給了鐵匠神，但她十分風流，與很多神如主神 Zeus 宙斯、戰神 Ares 阿瑞斯都有性愛關係，英文字如 aphrodisiac（催情藥）、venereal（性愛的、性慾的）、venery（縱慾）、venereal disease（性病）都源自 Aphrodite / Venus。🔁

Arachne (transformed into a spider)

Arachne（阿拉克涅）是古希臘神話的織女，編織特別著名，惹來工藝女神 Athena 雅典娜妒忌，最後，Athena 把她變為一隻蜘蛛，一生一世編織蜘蛛網，這故事在羅馬詩人 Ovid 奧維德的 *Metamorphoses*《變形記》也有提及。

Arachnid 是蜘蛛的生物學的學名，arachnida 即蛛形網，指節肢動物，如蜘蛛、蠍和蜱蟎。Arachne 則是 Marvel（漫威漫畫）角色"蜘蛛女"的別名。🔁

Asclepius (god of medicine)

Asclepius（阿斯克勒庇俄斯），是古希臘神話的 god of medicine（醫神），是太陽神 Apollo（阿波羅）和 Thessaly（塞薩利國）公主 Coronis（科洛尼斯）的兒子。Coronis 懷孕時，愛上凡人 Ischys（伊希斯），Apollo 憤怒之下叫孿生妹妹 Artemis（阿耳忒彌斯）射死 Coronis，在火化屍體時，Apollo 取出胎兒 Asclepius，交給半人馬 Chiron（喀戎）撫養。Chiron 教他醫術和狩獵，因此，Asclepius 的醫術特別出色，救人無數，但主神 Zeus（宙斯）怕他令人長生不死，所以用雷霹死 Asclepius。人類奉 Asclepius 為醫神，Zeus 為了安撫 Apollo，亦把 Asclepius 升為神。

Staff of Aesculapius（阿斯克勒庇俄斯之杖），又稱蛇杖，是醫神之手杖，是西方醫學界象徵醫術的標誌。世界衞生組織的旗幟亦有蛇杖圖。蛇杖的木棒象徵人類的脊骨，蛇則象徵復原和更新，因為蛇每年冬眠後會蛻換新皮。🔁

Asthma 哮喘

Asthma（哮喘），源於希臘文 *aazein*，意思是 "開口呼吸"，最早見於荷馬史詩 *Iliad*（《伊利亞特》，或《木馬屠城記》）。其中特洛依王子 Hector（赫克托爾）出現 "呼吸困難並吐血" 的現象。Hector 是特洛依城邦的善戰王子，因為殺死了 Achilles 的表弟 Patroclus 帕特羅克洛斯，最終遭 Achilles 殺死。

其後的古希臘典籍如 *Hippocrates Corpus*《醫神之書》，亦曾提及醫學名詞 Asthma，都是形容呼吸困難和咳嗽等病徵。🔁

Atlas

Atlas 阿特拉斯，古希臘神話的擎天神，是 Titan（泰坦）巨人神的第二代男神，是 Prometheus（普羅米修斯）的兄弟。他跟隨其他巨人神反抗宙斯，因而被罰在世界最西的地方用頭、肩頂住天（及地球）。

> 你知道嗎
> DO YOU KNOW?
>
> Atlas 即現在地理學的地圖。Atlas 又是醫學名詞，即第一頸椎，又稱寰椎，撐住頭部，如古希臘神 Atlas 般撐住天和地球。🔁

Cancer 癌 (a term first used by Hippocrates)
Cancer: ulcer forming tumor, oncologist

Cancer（癌）是古希臘醫學大師 Hippocrates（希波克拉底）首先使用，源於希臘文 *carcinos*，意思是 non-ulcer forming tumor（非潰瘍之腫瘤），以及 *carcinoma*，意思是 ulcer forming tumor（潰瘍之腫瘤）。

亦有人認為這字和希臘文 *oncos*（swelling，腫脹）有關，所以 "腫瘤學家" 是 oncologist。後來學者把 *carcinos* 轉為英文的 cancer。🔁

Cardio- [希臘文意思是心 (heart)]
Cardi- 意思是 pertaining to the heart
Latinized form of Greek kardia 意思是心 (heart)
Cardiothoracic 心臟與胸腔

Derma 皮膚 (skin)
Derma: dermatology, dermatologist, dermatosis, dermatitis, dermatography, dermoid, dermatoid, dermatophyte

Derma 是拉丁文，意思是 "皮膚 (skin)"。很多英文字，尤其是醫學名詞，都源於這個字，如：dermatology 是 "（醫學）皮膚科"，dermatologist 是 "皮膚科醫生"，dermatosis 是 "（醫學）皮膚病"，dermatitis 是 "（醫學）皮膚發炎"，dermatography 是 "（醫學）皮膚論"，dermoid 是 "皮膚構成的"，dermatoid 是 "皮狀的、皮樣的"，dermatophyte 是 "（醫學）皮膚真菌"。

很多美容產品、化粧品因為和皮膚有關,其洋名品牌多用上 *derma* 字眼。🔁

Diabetes 糖尿
Diabetes: Galen of Pergamon

Diabetes(糖尿),相傳古希臘醫學大師 Hippocrates(希波克拉底)發現及診斷出病人的尿有甜味。

另一位羅馬帝國的王室醫師 Galen of Pergamon(帕加馬的蓋侖),亦曾指 diabetes 是指"過量尿液"(*diarrhea urinosa*,excessive urinary output)。🔁

Diarrhea 肚瀉 (a term first used by Hippocrates)
Diarrhea: flowing through

Diarrhea 肚瀉,由古希臘醫學大師 Hippocrates(希波克拉底)首先使用,源於希臘文 *diarrhoia*,意指"flowing through",和食物、腸臟等疾病有關。

Hippocrates 又稱"醫學之父",最著名的是 Hippocratic Oath(希波克拉底的誓言),是醫生執行醫務前保證遵守醫生道德守則的誓言。🔁

Duodenum 十二指腸
拉丁文 *duodenum digitorium* 意思是 space of twelve digits

拉丁文 *duodeni*,意思是十二 (twelve),

希臘文 *dodekadaktylon*,意思是十二手指。

Genesis 創世紀 **(the first chapter of the Bible)**
Genesis: **gene, generate, generation,**
generator, genital, primogeniture

Genesis，即《聖經 · 舊約》中的第一章"創世紀"。

Vocabulary 延伸詞彙

源自 Genesis 的英文字有很多，以下是一些例子：gene（基因），
generate（產生），generation（世代、生殖），generator（發電、生殖
者），genital（生殖器官），primogeniture（封建社會的長子繼承制）。

⇄

Geron 希臘文意思是老人 **(old man)**

Gerontology 老人科

Gyno 希臘文意思是婦人 **(woman)**

Gynaecology 婦科

Hemo 希臘文意思是血 **(blood)**

法文 *hemo-*，
拉丁文 *haemo-*，
希臘文 *haimo-*，
Hemoglobin 是血色素，血紅蛋白。

Hepat 希臘文意思是肝 (liver)

hepatitis (n.) 肝炎：
希臘文 *hepatos*, genitive of hepar (liver)，
+ -itis 意思是發炎 (inflammation)。

hepatic (adj.)：
法文 *hepatique*，
拉丁文 *hepaticus*，
希臘文 *hepatikos* 意思是肝 (liver)。

Hermaphroditus 古希臘神話中的兩性神
Hermaphroditus: hermaphrodite brig, hermaphroditism

Hermaphroditus（赫耳瑪佛洛狄托斯）古希臘神話中的兩性神（god of hermaphrodite），象徵集兩性於一身，是信使神 Hermes（赫耳墨斯）和愛神 Aphrodite（阿佛洛狄忒）的兒子。他本來是一個英俊男子，但水仙女 Salmacis（薩爾瑪西斯）深愛他，緊抱他不肯分開，並求宙斯把他們結合在一起，因而成為集兩性性器官於一身的兩性體。

Vocabulary 延伸詞彙

生物學詞彙 hermaphrodite，即雌雄同體，在同性戀社區中亦廣泛使用；hermaphrodite brig，即半陰陽的，雌雄同株或同花蕊的，也解作雙桅帆船；hermaphroditism 即雌雄同體現象。🔄

Hygeia 古希臘神話中的醫神的女兒
Hygeia: hygiene, hygienic, hygienist

Hygeia 許革亞是古希臘神話中 god of medicine, Asclepius（醫神，阿斯克勒庇俄斯）的女兒，意思是 health（健康），所以她又稱為健康女神。她的形象是一個用碗餵蛇的少女。

Vocabulary 延伸詞彙

現有醫學名詞 hygiene、hygienic，都是衛生的意思；hygienic 即衛生學、保健學；hygienist 是衛生學家、保健專家，dental hygienist 即牙科洗牙師。🔄

Hymen 古希臘神話中的婚姻神 (god of marriage)
Hymen: hymenoptera, hymenopter, hymenotomy

Hymen（許門，Hymenaeus），古希臘神話中酒神 Dionysus（狄俄尼索斯）和愛神 Aphrodite（阿佛洛狄忒）的兒子，是 god of marriage（婚姻神）。

Vocabulary 延伸詞彙

Hymeno 是膜的意思，例如動物學的 hymenoptera（膜翅目）、hymenopter（膜翅目昆蟲）、hymen（處女膜）、以及醫學術語 hymenotomy（處女膜切開手術）。🔄

Hypertension 高血壓

hyper- 意思是高 (high)，+ tension，tension 意思是壓力 (pressure)。
Hypertension 意思是高血壓 (high blood pressure)。

Hypnos / Somnus 古希臘神話中的睡神 (Hypnos hynotized Zeus)

Hypnos: hypnogenesis, hypnotic, insomnia

Hypnos 許普諾斯是古希臘神話中的睡神，即羅馬神話的 Somnus。他長居於山洞內，洞外種滿罌粟和具催眠作用的植物。女主神 Hera（赫拉）曾請 Hypnos 催眠主神 Zeus（宙斯），令他長期入睡不去偷情，Hypnos 使用他的催眠術，令宙斯沉睡了一段時間。

Vocabulary 延伸詞彙

Hypnos 懂催眠術，所以英文 hypnogenesis 即催眠的意思。Hypnotic 就是安眠藥的意思。英文前綴 "in" 表示相反意義，所以，" 'in' - somnia" 是不能入睡的意思，失眠的病名就是叫 "insomnia"。

Iris 古希臘神話中的彩虹女神 (Rainbow)

Iris: Iridology, iris diagnosis, irisated, iris diaphragm

Iris 伊里斯是古希臘神話中的彩虹女神（Rainbow），通常在雨後出現，象徵 "風雨後的好現象"。《聖經・舊約》Noah's Ark（挪亞方舟）的故事中，四十日大洪水之後亦出現彩虹。

Vocabulary 延伸詞彙

現代醫學中，虹膜（iris）是環繞在眼睛瞳孔四周有色彩的部份，亦即表示我們的眼睛都有天堂的彩虹、瞳孔，研究這方面的醫學叫 iridology；透過虹膜去了解身體狀況叫 iris diagnosis（虹膜診斷）。iris 也解作 "鳶尾"，irisated 即彩虹色的，iris diaphragm 即 "虹彩光圈"，可調節進入鏡頭的光度。

Luna 月亮 (the moon)
Luna: Lunar, lunar calendar, lunar eclipse, lunatic, lunatic asylum

Luna 是拉丁文，意思是 "月亮 (the moon)"。源自 Selene 是希臘神話之月亮女神，羅馬則是 Luna。月亮不喜歡人看她，人如果長久看着月亮，會變成 lunatic (月癡)，即 "瘋子"。古時的人認為月圓之夜會出現 werewolf (人狼)，他們本來是狼，平時外型與常人無異，但在月圓之夜會變回狼形在山口呼叫，並侵襲人類。很多英文字都源於這個字，如：lunar 是 "月的"，lunar calendar 是 "農曆" (根據月亮運行的中國陰曆)，lunar eclipse 是 "月蝕"，lunatic 是 "精神病人、瘋子、月癡"，lunatic asylum 是 "瘋人院"。🔄

Mater 母親 (mother)
Mater: maternal, maternalize, maternity, maternity benefit, maternity nurse, maternity ward, matron, alma mater

Mater 是拉丁文，意思是 "mother (母親)"。很多英文字都源於這個字，如：maternal 是 "母親的"，maternalize 是 "成為母親"，maternity 是 "母親身份、母性"，maternity benefit 是 "產婦津貼"，maternity nurse 是 "助產士"，maternity ward 是 "產房"，matron 是 "資深護士長"，*alma mater* 是 "母校"。🔄

Morpheus 古希臘神話中睡神的兒子 (the son of the god of sleep)
Morpheus: morphine, morphinism, morphinize, morphinomania, morphinomaniac

Morpheus（摩耳甫斯），古希臘神話中睡神 Hypnos（許普諾斯，god of sleep）的兒子。

Vocabulary 延伸詞彙

現在的毒藥 morphine（嗎啡）乃源於他，有止痛、催眠的作用，但亦會上癮，所以是毒藥。其他衍生字包括：morphinism（嗎啡癮）、morphinize（用嗎啡治療、麻醉）、心理學名詞 morphinomania（嗎啡狂）、morphinomaniac（嗎啡狂者）。⇄

Narkissos: narcissus

Narkissos 古希臘神話中的美少年 (transformed to the narcissus)
Narkissos 那耳喀索斯，古希臘神話中的美少年，很多仙女也喜歡他，但都遭他拒絕，所以，愛神詛咒他愛上自己，終日在河邊看自己的倒影，直至死在河邊，成為水仙花（narcissus）。Narcissus（水仙花）就是古希臘神話中的"自戀狂"美少男。

Vocabulary 延伸詞彙

現代心理學家稱自戀症為 Narcissism。其他衍生字包括 narcotic（麻醉劑、致幻毒品）、narcotize（使昏迷）、narcotism（麻醉狀態）。Narkissos，古希臘文是 c，近現代多用 k。⇄

Nasci 出生 **(to be born)**
Nasci: **natal, prenatal, postnatal, natalism, natalist, neonate, neonatal, neonatal mortality, native, native land, native tongue**

Nasci 是拉丁文，意思是 "to be born（出生）"。
很多英文字都源於這個字，如：natal 是 "與出生有關、分娩的"，prenatal 是 "出生前"，postnatal 是 "出生後"，natalism 是 "鼓勵生育政策"，natalist 是 "鼓勵生育者"，neonate 是 "初生嬰兒"，neonatal 是 "新生兒的、新生期的"，neonatal mortality 是 "新生嬰兒死亡率"，native 是 "本土的、與生俱來的"，native land 是 "出生地"，native tongue 是 "天生的語言"。🔁

Naus 船 **(ship)**
Naus: **nautic, nautical, nautical almanac, nautical archaeology, nausea, naupathia**

Naus 是拉丁文，意思是 "ship（船）"。很多英文字都源於這個字，如：nautic 是 "水兵、水手"，nautical 是與 "船、海員、海哩有關的"，nautical almanac 是 "航海（天文）曆"，nautical archaeology 是 "航海考古學"，nausea 是 "暈船浪、嘔吐"(ship sickness)"，naupathia 是 "(醫學) 暈船"。🔁

Neuro 神經

neur- 或 *neuro-* 意思是 pertaining to nerves or the nervous system。

希臘文 *neuro-* 意思是神經 (nerve)。

Nyx 象徵 "黑夜" (the daughter of Chaos)
Nyx: nyctalgia, nyctalopia, nocturia

Nyx 倪克斯，在古希臘神話中象徵 "night (黑夜)"，是由 Chaos (卡俄斯，混沌) 所生的女神。Nyx 生下很多神，包括睡眠神 Hypnos (許普諾斯)、太空神 Aether (埃忒耳)、白晝神 Hemera (赫墨拉)、命數神 Moros (摩羅斯)、復仇神 Nemesis (涅墨西斯)、欺騙神 Apate (阿帕忒)、破壞神 Eris (厄里斯)。

Vocabulary 延伸詞彙

英文 night 源自 Nyx 的羅馬名字 *nox*。很多與晚間有關的病，亦以 *nycto* 或 *nocte* 為 prefix (字首)，如 nyctalgia (晚間疼痛)、nyctalopia (夜盲症)、nocturia (夜尿症)。有一安眠藥的牌子亦叫 Nox。

Oculus 眼睛的 (eye)
Oculus: oculist, ocular demonstration, ocularist, oculomotor, oculomotor nerve, oculonasal, monocle, binoculars

Oculus 是拉丁文，意思是 "eye (眼睛的)"。很多英文字都源於這個字，如：oculist 是 "眼科醫師、眼科學家、驗光師"，ocular demonstration 是 "可親眼目睹的實證"，

ocularist 是 "假眼製造商", oculomotor 是 "眼球運動的",
oculomotor nerve 是 "動眼神經", oculonasal 是 "眼鼻的",
monocle 是 "單鏡望遠鏡", binoculars 是 "（複數）兩鏡
（尤其是觀鳥用的）望遠鏡"。🔁

Oesophagus 食道：由喉到胃的部份 (is the part of the body that carries food from the throat to the stomach)

來自希臘文 *oisophagos*，*phagein* 意思是食 (to eat)。

Oncology 腫瘤科

onco- 意思是腫瘤 (tumor)，+ -logy 意思是 study of。
carcinoma 意思是潰瘍之腫瘤 (ulcer forming tumor)，
亦有人認為和希臘文 *oncos* (swelling，腫脹) 有關，所以
"腫瘤學家" 是 oncologist。
後來學者把 *carcinos* 轉為英文的 cancer（癌症）。🔁

Ophthalmology 眼科

希臘文 *ophthalmos* 的意思是眼 (eye)。

Osteoporosis 骨質疏鬆

希臘文 osteo- 的意思是骨 (bone)。
+ stem of 希臘文 *poros*，意思是 passage、voyage。

Pan 是古希臘神話中的牧神 (god of shepherds)
Pan: panic, panic disorder

Pan 潘恩，是古希臘神話中的 god of shepherds（牧神），掌管森林、田地和牲畜。他樣貌怪異，半人半獸，長着人的頭和身體、山羊的腿蹄、角和耳，當他出現時，很多人都會恐慌。

Vocabulary 延伸詞彙

因為潘恩的怪異樣貌往往令人感到恐懼，所以英文 panic（恐慌）源於 Pan，醫學上的恐慌症亦稱 panic disorder。🔄

Panacea (goddess of remedy)
Panacea: Asclepius, Hygeia

Panacea 帕那刻亞是古希臘神話中的治療女神 (goddess of remedy)，是醫神 (Asclepius, god of medicine) 的女兒，妹妹包括 Hygeia (Hygiene 衛生)。

你知道嗎
DO YOU KNOW?
現在英文 panacea 有 "靈丹妙藥、萬能藥、萬應藥、秘藥、社會弊病的補救方法" 的意思。🔄

Parere 產子 (to give birth to)
Parere: parents, parental, parenthood, parentage, parent company, parenting, parenticide

Parere 是拉丁文，意思是 "to give birth to（產子）"。很多英文字都源於這個字，如：parents 是 "父母"，parental 是 "父母的"，parenthood 是 "家長身份"，parentage 是 "出

身、家系、門第"，parent company 是 "母公司、總公司"，
parenting 是 "對孩子的養育"，parenticide 是 "殺父母"。
🔁

Phalanx 方陣、手指、腳趾骨
Phalanx: Macedonia

Phalanx 是古希臘文，源於古希臘 Macedonia（馬其頓）軍
隊的方陣，現在英文的意思包括：軍事的密集隊、密集的人
羣及（醫學 / 解剖學）的手指骨和腳趾骨。

> ### 你知道嗎
> #### DO YOU KNOW?
> Phalanx 雖然源於古希臘軍隊的方陣，但可能由於形狀的原因，
> 於現代醫學或解剖學裏，是人體的手指和腳趾骨的名詞。🔁

Pharmacy [pharmac, 希臘文的意思是藥 (drug, medication)]
藥劑學拉丁文 *pharmacia*

希臘文 pharmakeia 意思是 use of drugs, medicines, potions,
remedy, cure
pharmakeus (fem. 則是 pharmakis)，意思是製藥者 (preparer
of drugs)

Priapus 男性生殖力之神 (the son of Dionysus and Aphrodite)
Priapus: priapic, priapically, priapism

Priapus（普里阿普斯），古希臘神話中酒神 Dionysus（狄俄
尼索斯）和愛神 Aphrodite（阿佛洛狄忒）之子，是男性生殖
力之神，所以又是男性的陰莖的意思。

形容詞 priapic (偉男的，陽剛的) 及副詞 priapically 乃源自酒神 Priapus。醫學名詞 priapism，即陰莖異常勃起，也解作淫蕩行為或好色。⇄

Rumpere 破裂 (to break)
Rumpere: corrupt, disrupt, disruptive, interruption, interruptive, rupture, erupt, eruption, eruptive

Rumpere 是拉丁文，意思是 "to break（破裂）"。很多英文字都源於這個字，如：corrupt 是 "破壞、貪污"，disrupt 是 "破裂的、分裂的、破壞性的、製造混亂的"，interruption 是 "中止、間斷"，interruptive 是 "打斷的、打擾的"，rupture 是 "破裂、裂開、決裂、斷絕"，erupt（動詞）、eruption（名詞）、eruptive（形容詞）是 "爆發、突然發生、（醫學）出疹、出牙"。⇄

Skopein 請參看 (to see, look)

Skopein: telescope, microscope, horoscope, periscope, kaleidoscope, kinetoscope, endoscope, endoscopy

Skopein 是拉丁文，意思是 "to see, look（看）"。很多英文字都源於這個字，如：telescope 是 "望遠鏡"，microscope 是 "顯微鏡"，horoscope 是 "觀星學"，periscope 是 "潛水鏡"，kaleidoscope 是 "萬花筒"，kinetoscope 是 "早期的電影放映機"，endoscope 是 "內窺鏡"，endoscopy 是 "內窺鏡檢查"，colonoscopy 是 "腸鏡"。⇄

Tantalus 永遠喝不到嘴下的水 (the son of Zeus)
Tantalus: tantalize, tantalization, tantalizer, tantalizing,
Tantalum, Tantalus

Tantalus（坦塔羅斯），古希臘神話中 Zeus 宙斯之子，但因為洩露天機，被罰在池水中，頭上有葡萄卻在鼻尖上，他越是盡力伸長脖子，葡萄越會上升，使他永遠吃不到；他越是盡力垂下頭，水越會退下，使他永遠喝不到嘴下的水。

Vocabulary 延伸詞彙

動詞 tantalize（逗引）、名詞 tantalization（可望而不可即之苦）、tantalizer（誘惑者、引逗他人者）以及 tantalizing（若即若離的心理狀況、忐忑）都源於 Tantalus。

> **你知道嗎**
> **DO YOU KNOW?**
> 香港中文大學醫學院的一個探測糖尿機器也以 Tantalum 為名，太多或太少糖都會使它響起警號。此外，Tantalus 也衍生出化學元素如 Tantalum（化學元素鉭，Ta）。⇄

Thalassa 象徵 "大海" (the daughter of Aether and Hemera)
Thalassa: Thalassemia

Thalassa 塔拉薩，古希臘神話中天神保護牆 Aether 埃忒耳和 Hemera 赫墨拉的女兒，象徵 "大海"，亦是地中海的化身。她和大海 Pontus 薩托斯結合，生了九個半人半水獺的生物，是羅德島 Rhodes 第一批居民。

> **你知道嗎**
> **DO YOU KNOW?**
> Thalassemia（地中海貧血症）是醫學上的一種遺傳性血病，最早見於地中海。⇄

Ulcer (n.) 潰瘍

法文 *ulcere*，

拉丁文 *ulcerem*，

拉丁文 *ulcus*，意思是潰瘍的 (ulcer, a sore)，

希臘文 *elkos*，意思是潰瘍 (a wound, sore, ulcer)。

Urology 泌尿科

意思是尿 (urine)。

希臘文 *ouron*，意思是尿 (urine)。

Vito 生命 (life-giving)
Vito: vital, vitality, vitalize, vitalist, vitamin, C.V., Vito

Vito 是拉丁文，意思是 "生命 (life-giving)"。很多英文字都源於這個字，如：vital 是 "生命的、至關重要的"，vitality 是 "生命力、生機、活力"，vitalize 是 "使有生命、生氣"，vitalist 是 "生機論者"，vitamin 是 "維生素"，C.V. 即 *curriculum vitae*，意思是 "履歷"，即 "生命的記錄"，Vito (維托) 是男子名字。⇄

Names and abbreviations of chemicals
from Greek / Latin
來自希臘文 / 拉丁文的化學元素

Actinium (Greek: *Aktis*) [古希臘文 c 與 k 相通]，所以簡寫是 **Ac**
Aluminium (Latin: *Alumen*)，所以簡寫是 **Al**
Argon (Greek: *Argon*)，所以簡寫是 **Ar**
Calcium (Greek / Latin: *Calx*)，所以簡寫是 **Ca**
Carbon (Latin: *Carbo, Carbone*)，所以簡寫是 **C**
Cerium (Latin: *Ceres*)，所以簡寫是 **Ce**
Chlorine (Greek: *Chloros*)，所以簡寫是 **Cl**
Copper (Greek / Latin: *Cuprum*)，所以簡寫是 **Cu**
Dysprosium (Greek: *Dysprositos*)，所以簡寫是 **Dy**
Europium (Greek: *Europe*)，所以簡寫是 **Eu**
Gold (Latin: *Aurum*)，所以簡寫是 **Au**
Hafnium (Latin: *Hafnia*)，所以簡寫是 **Hf**
Helium (Latin: *Helios*)，所以簡寫是 **He**
Indium (Greek: *Indikon*, Latin: *Indicum*)，所以簡寫是 **In**
Iodine (Greek: *Iodes*)，所以簡寫是 **I**
Iron (Latin: *Ferrum*)，所以簡寫是 **Fe**
Lead (Latin: *Plumbum*)，所以簡寫是 **Pb**
Lithium (Greek: *Lithos*)，所以簡寫是 **Li**
Magnesium (Greek: *Magnesia*)，所以簡寫是 **Mg**
Mercury (Greek / Latin: *Hydragyrum* [*Hydor* and *argyros* = water and silver]; *Hydra* 是希臘神話的水蛇 ; *Argyrum* = *Argentum* = **silver = Ag)**，所以簡寫是 **Hg**
Molybdenum (Greek: *Molybdos*)，所以簡寫是 **Mo**

Neon (Greek: *Neos*)，所以簡寫是 Ne

Neptunium (Latin: *Neptunus*)，所以簡寫是 Np

Niobium (Greek: *Niobe*)，所以簡寫是 Nb

Nitrogen (Greek / Latin: *Nitrum, genes*)，所以簡寫是 N

Oxygen (Greek: *Oxygene*)，所以簡寫是 O

Phosphorus (Greek / Latin: *Phos, Phoros*)，所以簡寫是 P

Platinum (Latin: *Platina*)，所以簡寫是 Pt

Plutonium (Latin: *Pluto*)，所以簡寫是 Pu

Potassium (Latin: *Kalium*)，所以簡寫是 K

Promethium (Greek: *Prometheus*)，所以簡寫是 Pm

Radium (Latin: *Radius*)，所以簡寫是 Ra

Rhenium (Latin: *Rhenus*)，所以簡寫是 Re

Rhodium (Greek: *Rhodon*)，所以簡寫是 Rh

Ruthenium (Latin: *Ruthenia*)，所以簡寫是 Ru

Scadium (Latin: *Scandia*)，所以簡寫是 Sc

Selenium (Greek: *Selene*)，所以簡寫是 Se

Silicon (Latin: *Silex*)，所以簡寫是 Si

Silver (Latin: *Argentum*)，所以簡寫是 Ag

Sodium (Greek: *Nitron,* Latin: *Natrium*)，所以簡寫是 Na

Sulfur (Latin: *Sulpur, Sulphur, Sulfur*)，所以簡寫是 S

Tantalum (Greek: *Tantalus*)，所以簡寫是 Ta

Tellurium (Latin: *Tellus*)，所以簡寫是 Te

Tin (Latin: *Stannum*)，所以簡寫是 Sn

Titanium (Greek: *Titan*)，所以簡寫是 Ti

Uranium (Greek / Latin: *Uranus*)，所以簡寫是 U

Xenon (Greek: *Xenox*)，所以簡寫是 Xe

Mottoes (in Greek / Latin and English translation)
來自希臘文 / 拉丁文的校訓 / 格言 / 座右銘

Ad maiorem Dei gloriam
(To the greater glory of God) – The Jesuit Order
Artes, scientia, veritas
(Arts, science, truth) – University of Michigan
Benedicere, laudare, praedicare
(To bless, to praise, and to preach) – The Dominican Order
Citius, altius, fortius
(Swifter, higher, stronger) – The Olympic motto
Disciplina praesidium civitatis
(The instruction and protection of the state) – University of Texas
Domino optimo maximo
(To the Lord, best and greatest) – The Benedictine Order
Dominus illuminatio mea
(The Lord is my light) – Oxford University
Fiat lux
(Let there be light) – University of California
Hinc lucem et pocula sacra
From whence issue light and the sacred draughts of wisdom) – Cambridge University
In Deo speramus
(In God we trust) – Brown University
Ingenio et labore
(By natural ability and hard work) – University of Auckland
Labor omnia vincit
(Work conquers all) – University of Illinois
Lux et veritas
(Light and truth) – Yale University
Veritas
(Truth) – Harvard University

References
參考書目

The Penguin Dictionary of Quotations. Edited by J.M. and M.J. Cohen (London: Penguin, 1960).

The Anchor Book of Latin Quotations with English Translations. Compiled by Norbert Guterman. (New York: Anchor Books, 1990).

Aesop: The Complete Fables. Translated by Olivia and Robert Temple. (London: Penguin, 1998).

Lend Me Your Ears: Great Speeches in History. Edited by William Safire. (New York: W.W. Norton, 2004).

《拉丁成語辭典》*A Dictionary of Latin Proverbs* (Latin-English-Chinese) Edited by Leopold Leeb. (北京：宗教文化出版社，2006).

It's Not Greek to Me —《必學英文 100 經典名句》Jeremy & Sara Walenn 著 (香港：商務，2011).

《異口同聲 *Be of One Voice*：中英成語 800 對》(修訂版) 陳永禎、陳善慈編著 (香港：商務，2011).

《字源學英文》張學明編著 (香港：商務，2017).

《中西神話》張學明編著 (香港：中華，2012).